I0535813

Sammy in England

Single Wide Female Travels
Book 4

By

Lillianna Blake

DEDICATION

To all women out there who are facing
your fears – you got this! ☺

TABLE OF CONTENTS

CHAPTER 1..7

CHAPTER 2.. 11

CHAPTER 3.. 17

CHAPTER 4.. 23

CHAPTER 5.. 29

CHAPTER 6.. 35

CHAPTER 7.. 41

CHAPTER 8.. 47

CHAPTER 9.. 51

CHAPTER 10 55

CHAPTER 11 61

CHAPTER 12 67

CHAPTER 13 73

CHAPTER 14 79

CHAPTER 15 85

CHAPTER 16 91

CHAPTER 17 95

CHAPTER 18 101

CHAPTER 19 107

CHAPTER 20 111

CHAPTER 21 117

CHAPTER 22 123

CHAPTER 23 127

CHAPTER 24 133

CHAPTER 25 139

CHAPTER 26 145

CHAPTER 27 151

CHAPTER 28 155

CHAPTER 29 159

CHAPTER 30 165

CHAPTER 1

I sighed and smiled as Max's fingertip swirled a lazy pattern along my palm. With the sun just setting, the scenery outside the train window had me captivated. The subtle rhythm of the train, combined with the sensation of Max's touch, had lulled me into such a peaceful state that I couldn't be worried about our arrival in London. After what had happened in Amsterdam, what could be worse?

I glanced over at Max to see him staring at the seat in front of him.

"Max, you're missing all the scenery."

"Sorry." He smiled and looked out the window. "It is beautiful."

"This entire journey has been amazing, and now I'm looking forward to meeting one of your good friends."

"Good friend is a little strong. We knew each other as kids—for a summer."

"Hm, I bet she has some good stories about you." I

grinned.

"Never mind that." He cut his eyes in my direction. "No teasing."

"Why not? I never get to tease you."

He leaned close and kissed me on the cheek. "I'm looking forward to having a romantic evening with you—just the two of us."

"Me too." I gazed into his eyes. Valentine's Day was coming up, and it still shocked me at times that I had the privilege of sharing it—and all the other special events that used to drive me insane as a chronically single woman—with Max. Never did I think that fantasy would come true. But there he was, right before me, smiling at me, as if he felt as lucky as I did. "I love you, Max."

"I love you too." He stroked his palm across mine. "But you're not getting me back in a storage container."

"Don't worry, I already checked on that. I didn't want any surprises like what we had in Amsterdam. Poppy has us set up at a lovely bed and breakfast where we can stay for the duration of our visit."

"That should be nice. I'm sure it'll still be a small room, but at least we'll have a bathroom."

"I hope so." I laughed and leaned into his shoulder. "I'm not sure I'm brave enough to go without one again."

"It's not bravery, trust me." He chuckled and wrapped his arm around my waist. "At least she's a little more forthcoming with our plans."

"Yes, she's already e-mailed me an hour-by-hour

event plan for the first few days. She even scheduled time for a shower for me." I grinned. "I don't think she's going to be full of surprises." I bit into my bottom lip lightly. "I do feel bad that I've made such a bad impression."

"What do you mean?"

"The incident with the hot air balloon..." I cringed.

"So what? That wasn't your fault."

"Maybe not to you or me, but I think to Poppy, it was. Anyway, I'm not going to focus on that. I can't let someone's opinion of me get me derailed. I'm sure we'll still have a fantastic time in London."

Max glanced at his watch. "We should be there in an hour."

"I'm going to work on my blog a bit. I've been neglecting it. Plus, I want to read back through some old posts. Do you mind?"

"Not at all." He kissed the top of my head. "I'm going to get a little rest."

I opened my computer, happy to see that the train Wi-Fi service seemed to be working. As soon as I logged onto my blog, I saw a flood of comments. My eyes widened at some of the more colorful ones.

SWF how many calories were in that cookie?

SWF when are you coming back to Italy?

SWF how can you travel so much? Aren't you working on the next book in the series? We can't wait forever.

I laughed and started typing out responses.

Twenty minutes passed before I even had the chance to look at some old posts. I decided to go back to the first few posts I'd ever made. When I started reading back through my initial plans for my bucket list, I was stunned.

I'd been filled with so much fear and excitement at that time in my life. More than anything, though, I recognized the extreme amount of determination I'd had. It was clear to me that over the span of my travels I'd became blind to my true passion. A few reminders would be a good way to get myself back on track.

I titled my new blog post *Back to Basics* and began typing away. By the time I hit the submit button, the train had rolled into the London station.

I glanced over at Max to see that his eyes were still open. He hadn't slept at all.

"Max?" I grabbed his hand before he could stand up and retrieve our luggage. "Are you doing okay?"

"Sure." He smiled at me. "Let's check out London."

CHAPTER 2

I followed Max off the train along with several other passengers. Though it was already dark when we stepped out onto the street, the city was well lit. I waved down a taxi. Max tossed the suitcases in the trunk then joined me in the warmth of the back seat.

"Summer Inn please." I handed the driver the address.

"Is that where you're staying?" He looked over his shoulder at us.

"Yes. Do you know it?"

He chuckled. "Sure do. That place is booked to the attic."

"Wow. Must be a nice place."

"It's because of the rumor about it."

"Rumor?" I leaned forward to listen as the driver pulled away from the curb.

"With Valentine's Day coming up, people are tripping all over themselves to get a room there. Supposedly a great love story took place there."

"That sounds wonderful. I didn't know anything about that."

"It's more of a local superstition. Anyway, lots of couples like to stay there for good luck in their relationship."

"That's sweet, but how could an inn offer good luck?"

"It's not the Inn, it's the initials. The building is an old Victorian style, and when it was being renovated a few years back, one of the workers discovered a pair of initials engraved underneath the railing of the porch. Historians dated it back hundreds of years."

"Oh wow, how amazing. Love does endure."

"Yes, I guess the owner thought so too. So she insisted that the wood remain a part of the railing. Then she researched who the couple might have been. There's no way to prove it, of course, but supposedly the couple was Sarah Martin and Thomas Whittle. Sarah Martin was the daughter of a very well-off and powerful man in England. Thomas Whittle was listed as a farm hand, nothing more than a cattle herder, most likely. The story goes that Sarah tried to get her father to agree to their marriage. Her father refused and had Thomas arrested. Sarah sat outside of the jail until he was released. The two fled and likely holed up in the house to escape her father's wrath."

"And they lived happily ever after?" Max grinned. "That's my kind of story."

"Actually, no one really knows." The driver looked in the rear-view mirror at me. "The last time either was seen they were on the porch of that house. Sarah's father hunted for them but never found them. Some people believe they ran off together, others believe Sarah's father murdered them both, and some suspect that, tired of running, Sarah and Thomas jumped into the river."

"Wow, that's not so pleasant." Max shook his head. "I despise stories like that."

"Really?," I asked. "Don't you think it's beautiful that they loved one another so much?"

"It's a story, Sammy. There's no way to prove if it's true or not. Such a tragic one at that. I hate to think of anyone being killed, or killing themselves over love." Max shook his head. "There's nothing beautiful to me about that."

"Not even how deeply they loved each other?" I met his eyes.

"Love is beautiful, but it's not meant to be violent." He frowned. "I never understood those kinds of sad movies. Love should be inspiring and uplifting, not horrifying."

"I guess it doesn't work out that way for everyone." The driver smiled as he pulled up in front of the bed and breakfast. "Anyway, good luck with the crowd, and have a wonderful time in London."

I stepped out of the taxi and waited for Max to collect

the luggage. The railing held my attention. I wondered if the story was true. Did two lovers from so long ago leave their mark for everyone to see forever? It was an amazing thought.

I took one of the suitcases from Max and slipped my hand into his free one.

"Do you think it's true, Max?"

"I kind of hope not."

"Why?" I looked into his eyes.

"The thought of someone having to endure that kind of pain—it makes me feel sorry for them."

"But obviously their love was stronger than that pain. Maybe that made it worth it."

"Maybe." Max shrugged and made his way up the steps to the front door. He held it open for me.

As I stepped past him, it struck me that Max might not believe in that powerful kind of love. I had no problem believing in it, because I experienced it every moment that I was with him. Did that mean that he didn't experience the same thing? *Nonsense, Sammy, Max just has a more logical mind. Don't ruin things by overthinking it.* I willed myself to keep control of my emotions.

The lobby was crowded, and the woman at the front desk looked as if she hadn't slept in days.

"Maybe this isn't the best place for us to stay." I frowned.

"We're going to have to give it a try tonight. It's too late to find anywhere else. If it's this bad in the morning,

14

we can find somewhere else to stay."

"Good, logical plan, Max." I nudged him with my elbow.

"Thanks..." He grinned. "I'm looking forward to getting some sleep."

I walked up to the counter when I saw that the woman at the desk was free. Her name tag said Madison.

"Hello, I'm checking in."

"Oh, Samantha, no need to explain. I know just who you are." She grinned. "I'm so thrilled to have you staying here. When Poppy mentioned you were going to be in London, I begged her to reserve your room here."

"Really?" I smiled. "That's quite kind of you."

"I have to admit that I had a reason—well, other than being your biggest fan."

"What's that?" I signed the logbook.

"I thought that maybe you'd like to include something about the Inn and its tragic love story in your next book. What better inspiration than a romantic story like that?"

"Well, I don't really write romance."

"Of course not, but love is always a part of everything, isn't it?" She smiled. "Just think about it. I don't expect you to answer me now."

"Alright, I will." I smiled at her and accepted our room keys.

15

CHAPTER 3

Max cringed as we walked away from the counter.

"We'll have to be careful of her."

"Madison? Why?"

"She seems a bit determined to get into your next book."

"I think it's sweet."

"Maybe, but there's no way you could use a story like that in your book."

"Why not?" We climbed the stairs to the second floor.

Max paused on the landing. "Because, like you said, you don't write romance. You write inspiration."

"Romance can be inspiring. Madison is right—love is part of everything. Without love, you can't really have happiness."

Max was silent as he waited for me to open the door to our room.

I turned to look at him. "Don't you think so, Max?"

"Honestly?" He met my eyes.

"Honestly." I nodded.

"No, I don't think that's true. Love is great, but not everyone has to have it to be happy."

I tried not to let his words skewer me through the heart. He was entitled to his opinion of course.

"So, if we weren't together, you'd be happy?"

"Sammy, that's not fair. Don't put words in my mouth." Max eyed me warily. "Can we just go into the room?"

I nodded and stepped inside.

The room was fairly big, with a queen-sized bed, side tables, and a small kitchen table. I noticed right away that there was a rather large painting on one wall depicting a rose in full bloom.

"Look at that." I smiled at the image. "It's breathtaking."

Max nodded and set his suitcase down beside the bed. I noticed that he'd barely looked at the painting.

"Max, really—look at it."

He sighed and sat down on the edge of the bed. "It's a rose, Sammy. It's just a rose."

Something about the way he said it made my eyes widen and my heart flip. Where was my Max that usually shared my passion for everything? Where was the man that, at the very least, supported my views?

"Max, are you sure you're okay?"

"I'm just tired." He yawned. "I'm sorry. I guess I'm a little cranky."

"It's okay." I smiled and sat down beside him. "Why

don't you head to bed? I want to check in on the blog to see if I have any comments, then I'll be going to bed myself."

"Okay." He yawned again. Then he reached over and wrapped his arms around me. "Don't be long. I don't sleep well without you."

I kissed him gently. "Not long at all, I promise."

I set my computer up on the small table and settled in for some reading.

One thing that I'd noticed about my adventures with my bucket list was my hesitation and avoidance when it came to physical activity. It was strange to look back on that, because I'd learned to really enjoy being more active. But I hadn't been that active lately. Maybe that was why some anxiety had begun creeping back into my daily life. I'd discovered that the physical body was meant to be used, designed for far more activity than the convenient lifestyle modern society offered.

I typed up a blog post about how easy it was to lose sight of the needs of the body. Even while focusing on emotional and spiritual needs, it was easy to overlook the fact that we are physical beings, who need to be exercised just like any other animal.

When I crawled into bed beside Max, I was determined to show more respect to my physical being, even if being warm and cozy cuddled up next to Max seemed like a much better idea.

I woke up the next morning feeling more like myself than I had in a very long time. I tickled Max's neck until he stirred awake.

"Want to go for a run with me?"

"A run?" He stared at me with wide eyes. "Seriously?"

"Yes. I feel like running. Do you want to join me?"

"Sure do." He climbed out of bed. "What brought this on?"

"It's been so long since I've done anything physical. I think I've built up some anxiety and aggression because of it. I just feel like running to the ends of the earth and letting off some steam."

"I think that's a great idea. Give me a second to change."

I rummaged through my suitcase for some running gear. With my fluctuating schedule, exercise had fallen to the wayside. Sure, we were active as we explored the different places we'd been visiting, but it wasn't the same as pure exercise. My body craved it, and so did my psyche.

Reading over those first few blog posts, about how difficult it had been for me to get motivated to exercise, reminded me that I didn't want to slide back to that place again. I liked the adrenaline that came from a good workout and the clarity of thought that followed. It wasn't that I'd gotten lazy, just busy and neglectful of my physical needs.

"Ready?" Max smiled and pulled me into a tight hug.

"Ready! I'll race you to the end of the block."

"Oh, you think you can beat me, do you?"

"Loser buys breakfast." I rushed out the door of the room and down the stairs with Max right on my heels.

When I burst out the door onto the sidewalk, I was surprised by the change in temperature.

"Yikes, I'm going to have to work up a sweat."

"Sammy, wait! Be careful!"

I ignored Max's warning and ran as fast as I could toward the end of the block. I could see a small restaurant. It beckoned to me through the pedestrians and traffic. I could hear Max a few steps behind me. Despite the rhythm of his footsteps, I suspected that he slowed his pace in order to let me win. I looked back over my shoulder.

"I know you can run faster than that, Max! Move it!"

"Sammy!" Max pointed past me.

I turned in time to see a food cart pushed out onto the sidewalk, but not in time to stop myself from running into it. In a futile attempt to save myself, I jumped up as high as I could. For a split second I straddled the food cart, then I crashed right down on top of it, tipping the entire thing over.

Hot dog juices flooded my body from head to toe and created a large puddle on the sidewalk. The cart owner shrieked and struggled with the cart. Max tried to skid to a stop beside the cart, but his shoes slipped in the

21

hot dog juice puddle. His legs flew up into the air and he crashed down onto the sidewalk right beside me.

"Sammy, are you okay?" He groaned as he struggled to his feet.

CHAPTER 4

I managed to stand with the greasy water dripping off my body.

Max offered his shoulder for me to lean on.

"Who is going to pay for this? You are going to pay for this!" The owner of the hot dog cart jabbed his finger at me. "Why weren't you watching where you were going? You think it's so important to get where you're going? You've ruined my business for the entire day!"

"Here, let me help you." Max pulled the cart back up on to its wheels. Then he handed the man a business card. "Just contact me here and we'll settle things. Alright?"

"Crazy tourists!" The man shoved the card into his pocket and rolled the cart away.

"Oh my God, I can't believe this." I squeezed out the bottom of my shirt.

"Hey, things happen." Max cleared his throat.

"Don't you mean that you told me to slow down?"

"I didn't say that." Max met my eyes.

"You don't have to." I sighed. "I wasn't paying attention."

"Sammy, it's not a big deal. As long as you're not hurt, it's just something to laugh about."

"Don't you mean, I'm just something to laugh at?" I shook my head. "I don't think I'm hurt, but I'm going to need to go back to the room shower and change before I can get to the meeting with Poppy."

"Alright, let's head back." Max slid his hand into mine.

I appreciated the fact that he was willing to hold my hand despite the fact that it was covered with hot dog juice. Even as my clothes hung down from my body with the weight of the water, Max walked beside me just as proud as ever.

I remembered my doubts the night before—about whether he loved me as deeply as I loved him. When he looked over at me and winked, I didn't doubt him. He loved me even in my most embarrassing moments. I reorganized my thoughts and tried to focus on the positive. No one was hurt. Soon, I'd have a shower and be in clean clothes.

When we reached the Inn, there was a crowd of people outside the doors. The crowd was so thick that I couldn't even see the entrance.

"What is going on?" Max looked over the crowd.

I noticed a woman at the edge of the crowd and tapped her on the shoulder. When she turned to look at me she winced and drew back some.

"Do you know what's happening here?"

"Oh sure, a prince is here with his fiancée. They're trying to get good luck from the carving."

"Seriously?" Max shook his head. "He's a prince, isn't that good luck enough?"

The woman shrugged. "Everyone knows about it and wants to catch a glimpse of the prince."

"So, how do we get inside?"

"Oh, you don't." The woman laughed and pointed out several security officers that blocked the way into the Inn.

"Unbelievable." Max frowned. "We need to call Poppy."

"No, no really. It's fine." I took a deep breath. "I'm sure that they'll be leaving soon. It's sweet, really. And to think we're going to get a glimpse of royalty."

Max smiled. "You always see the bright side, Sammy."

"I try." I reached up and tried to brush the smelly liquid out of my hair.

After an hour slid by and my stomach rumbled for the hundredth time, I was not seeing much of a bright side.

"If I don't get in there soon, I'm not going to have time to shower or change. I can't meet Poppy like this."

"Can you call and postpone it?"

"No, I really can't. Poppy is a stickler for schedules."

"But I'm sure if you tell her what happened, she'll understand."

"No way, she can't know what happened. She already thinks I'm a little crazy. I don't want to confirm it for her."

"Alright." Max shoved his hands in his pockets. "Even if the prince leaves soon, this crowd is not going to clear out. I could try contacting the front desk, or we could just go buy you some new clothes."

"But the rest of me will still smell like hot dogs!" I frowned.

"Then we'll buy some new perfume too. It'll be a little shopping spree. You haven't had one of those for a while."

"True." I sighed. In the past shopping hadn't been my favorite thing to do, but now that I could fit into most of the sizes that stores offered, it was a little more fun. "But we have to shop fast or I'm going to be late."

"There's a store a few doors down this way." Max steered me around the crowd to the other side of the block.

I glanced back at the entrance of the Inn to see if I could catch a glimpse of the prince. All I saw were more security guards.

When we reached the shop my heart sank. It wasn't a traditional boutique but a specialty store that featured steampunk clothing—leather, chains, and funky colors.

"Hm, maybe not your style? Let's see what's further

up."

I looked at my watch, then shook my head. "No way, Max, I'm out of time. I'll have to find something in here."

"Alright." He swung the door open and grinned at the manikin in the window. "How about that? I like it."

I looked at the thin strap of leather that covered see-through lace and rolled my eyes. "I'm trying to make a good impression, Max, not show up naked."

"Hey, that always makes a good impression on me." Max winked.

I couldn't help but grin. Even in my most stressful moments Max could get a little laughter out of me.

CHAPTER 5

As I began to sort through the clothing on the rack, my amusement faded. I'd thought that there might be at least one plain t-shirt or blouse that could work, but everything was very funky and noticeable.

I finally came across a top that was mostly leather with some thin chains laced through it. It was still rather strange, but it would be more acceptable than the rest. I grabbed a pair of black leather trousers off the rack and carried the items to the counter.

The woman flipped a page in her magazine and looked up at me. "Are you sure you're in the right place?"

"Yes, I'd like to purchase these."

"Hm. Are you sure about that?"

"Yes. Please, I'm in a hurry." I put my credit card down on the counter.

"Look, there's a no-return policy. Do you want to try on the clothes?"

I narrowed my eyes. It was clear to me that the woman didn't think that I could fit into the clothing, but I'd checked the sizes and was confident that they would fit just fine.

"Please, just ring me up. I won't be returning them. I'm in a hurry, and I need to use your dressing room to change, if that's okay."

"Sure." She ran the credit card and handed it back to me. "Remember, no returns."

I tried not to glare at her. She was a very petite woman and perhaps she just assumed that anyone of a larger size shouldn't be wearing the style of clothing that she sold.

I rushed into the dressing room and changed out of my still-damp clothes. One whiff of my shirt told me that I'd made the right decision.

As I tugged on the new shirt, I tried not to look in the mirror. I was sure that I was going to look ridiculous. I still managed to catch a glimpse as I struggled into the leather pants. To my surprise, I thought the top fit me well. The pants were a little tight, but I only had to wear them for a little while.

When I stepped out of the dressing room Max whistled at me.

"Nice. I think I could get used to this style."

"Don't." I laughed. "It might work for me today, but there's no way I could pull this off all the time. But at least they fit." I shot a look in the clerk's direction. She didn't looked up from her magazine.

As we left the shop I checked my watch. "Ten minutes to get there. I think the bookstore is just a few blocks away."

"Okay, let's hurry." Max grabbed my hand and led me through the crowd on the sidewalk.

The small bookstore was on the corner of a block. Its front was rounded and stood out from the rest of the shops on the block. It had a sense of whimsy that reminded me of just how much I enjoyed a good book and a tucked-away place to read it.

"Page after Page." I smiled at the name of the shop. "Cute."

Max opened the door for me. I recognized Poppy right away from our meeting in Amsterdam.

"Hi, Poppy." I smiled.

"Samantha." She swept her gaze over my outfit, then looked back up at me. "I was wondering if you were coming."

"Oh, I didn't think I was late…" I frowned and glanced at my watch.

"You're not. I just try to make it a habit to be ten or fifteen minutes early."

I nodded. "That's a good habit."

"I think so."

"This is my husband, Max." I looked over at Max, who glanced up from a book he'd picked up from a shelf.

"Nice to meet you, Poppy."

"You too, Max." She smiled at him.

She didn't smile at me, but she sure didn't mind smiling at Max.

"Please, join me in my office, Samantha, and we can go over everything."

"Great." I followed her into her office.

It was a small space, but highly organized. Everything had a place. I knew this because there were labels placed in front of everything—pencil sharpener, pencils, paper, paper clips. It was a bit unsettling, but at the same time I could understand why someone would enjoy always knowing where everything was.

I sat down in the chair across from her and tried to hide the fact that I was looking for a label that said chair.

"I'm so glad that we're going to be working together, Poppy."

"Me too, Samantha. I just want to remind you that I run a very tight ship. I've found that as long as things happen the way they are supposed to, there is never any room for chaos."

"Okay." I smiled.

"We have a book signing in the evening tonight. I've paired it with a wine tasting and chosen a passage from the book for you to read. Please don't deviate from that passage. Just read it, and maybe a few questions and answers, then straight to mingling. Okay?"

"Sure." I bit into my bottom lip.

I tended to ramble off on my own topics during book signings. I was also used to choosing my own passage from the book to read. It seemed to me that Poppy really did want control of everything, but that was okay with me. I could use the break.

"Now tomorrow, I planned a tour through some local venues. Your fans can opt to purchase a ticket to join us on the tour. But please remember, this is not meant to be a free-for-all. I expect you to maintain professional behavior the entire time. Also, perhaps consider wearing something a bit more…" She paused and looked at my outfit again. "Mature."

"Yes, of course." My cheeks grew hot.

"What is that smell?" She sniffed the air. "Do you smell it too?"

I lowered my eyes.

"Samantha, do you smell it too?" She frowned. "It's awful. I'm going to have to speak to the cleaning lady."

"Is there anything else I should know?"

"Well, yes. Since you're here over Valentine's Day, I thought it might be good publicity for you to get involved in something a friend of mine is running. She owns a coffee shop and hosts poetry readings. For Valentine's Day, she's hosting a special event. It's a similar to speed dating, only her customers have to communicate solely through poetry. I think it's a bit silly, of course, but she's very excited about it. Anyway, she wants a few judges to rate the actual poetry and declare a winning couple at the end of the event. I suggested you as a judge—if you approve, of course."

"Oh, that sounds like a lot of fun. I'd love to do it."

"Great. I'll be there with you as well."

"Wonderful." I smiled. "Anything else?"

"Just be prepared for the event tonight, it starts promptly at six. Perhaps you could be early?" She pursed her lips. "And, I don't expect you not to drink, but it would be nice if you could limit yourself."

"Poppy, are you afraid I'm going to get drunk?"

"Should I be?"

CHAPTER 6

I stared at Poppy for a long moment. There were a few things I thought about saying to her, but I didn't want to further tarnish her image of me.

"Honestly, that's hurtful. I know that you have a poor impression of me, but I hope that you can be open to the thought that perhaps you have the wrong idea."

Poppy smiled at me in a way that made me think all was forgiven. Then she leaned across the table and looked directly into my eyes.

"So prove me wrong, darling."

My eyes widened. I wondered how I was going to survive working with this woman.

"I'll be there—early and sober." I stood up from my chair and narrowed my eyes. "You need to understand that I take my career very seriously. I'm a professional and soon you'll see that, Poppy." I turned to walk away from her.

"Well, I guess I'd rather see that than what I'm seeing right now." She made a sharp noise with her tongue. "If that's the kind of behavior I can expect tonight, then I doubt I have the wrong impression."

"What?" I looked over my shoulder at her. "What are you talking about?"

"Samantha, I don't know exactly how they do things in America, but I have never shown off my panties at a business meeting."

"What?" I looked down at my backside. Sure enough, my pink panties were easy to see through slits in the leather pants I was wearing.

The slits ran from below the waistband all the way to the back of my knees. I hadn't noticed them when I'd tried the pants on because I was in such a rush. All of a sudden I knew why the clerk had advised me against the clothes. I assumed it had been because she was judging my size. I didn't realize it was because she knew the pants were more revealing than I might like.

"I had no idea!" I frowned and tried to cover up the slits.

"Sure. You can go now. I'll see you tonight. And Samantha?"

I blinked back tears as I looked at her. "Yes?"

"Please try and take a shower. I'm not sure whether it's the perfume you're wearing or there's a hygiene problem, but I think it would be best if you washed up before the signing tonight."

"I will."

I hurried out of the office.

As embarrassment flooded me from the tips of my toes to the top of my head, I thought about all the people who'd likely seen my panties as Max and I had been rushing to get to the bookstore earlier. I thought about what Poppy must think of me.

I remembered what it was like to want to disappear.

"Sammy, you okay?" Max caught up with me at the door of the store.

"No, I'm not." I wiped at my eyes. "I'm awful. I just want to go back to the room. I don't care how much of a crowd or security issue there is—I need to shower and change."

"What happened? Was she rude?" He looked back into the shop toward where Poppy was stepping out of her office. "That woman needs to loosen up a little bit."

"Please, Max, let's just go. Can you walk behind me? Close?"

"Why?" Max looked down at my pants. "Oh no! Sammy, I swear I didn't see that."

"It's okay. I just want to go."

Max wrapped his arm around my waist and angled his body to cover most of my backside.

It was a long slow walk back to the Inn. Thankfully, when we arrived, the crowd of people was no longer there. Max escorted me up the steps into the Inn, then up the stairs to the second floor. When we reached the room, he opened the door for me.

"Do you want some company?" Max rubbed a hand

along my shoulder.

"Honestly, no. I'd really like to just change, shower, and then maybe read for a little while. I need to get my head out of this space for tonight."

"Okay, I'll head out, then. I'm just a phone call away if you need me. And Sammy?"

"Yes?" I turned to look at him.

"Don't let that woman get to you. Who is she to judge? It's not like she's leading a very happy life—well, she doesn't appear to be very happy, anyway."

"Thanks, Max." I smiled at him.

As soon as the door shut, I tore off my clothes. I stripped down to nothing and turned the water on in the bathtub. As the water ran, I thought about what Max had said. It was a little harsh, but he was only trying to help. Maybe he was right. Maybe Poppy was miserable.

I ran a fingertip through the warm water and closed my eyes. Over the years—especially the last few—I'd experienced so many embarrassing moments, but that meeting with Poppy was now near the top of the list.

Sure, she was a bit mean, but I knew that I needed to be able to work with all kinds of different people in order to reach them—no matter how closed off they appeared.

As I slid into the tub, I wondered just how closed off Poppy was. She seemed to be a fan of the book, yet everything about her was so rigid that I wondered how she could even enjoy my writing.

I closed my eyes and tried to think of ways that

Poppy and I were similar. It was a trick that I'd started using when I encountered someone that I didn't necessarily like very much right off the bat. I always found that if I could track down similarities between the other person and myself, I could gain an understanding so much faster..

Poppy liked things to go as planned, she liked to be in control, and she had high professional standards. Those were all things that I could identify with. Perhaps I wasn't as rigid as Poppy, but I did still struggle with my need for control, as that need was more of an anxiety than an actual need.

"She must be afraid to lose control." My eyes opened and I smiled. "That's it. She's more anxious than she is rigid. I just need to figure out why."

I thought about my earliest blog entries that I'd been rereading lately and an idea began to form in my mind. Maybe it was time for Poppy to experience her own bucket list.

Instead of avoiding Poppy, I was going to embrace her. I was going to be the best friend to her that Max had been to me for so many years. Poppy needed a chance to blossom, and I had plenty of experience when it came to stretching out petals.

CHAPTER 7

After my bath I curled up in bed with a book. Transported to another world, the muscles in my body relaxed and my mind calmed its frantic pace. There was little I enjoyed more than disappearing inside a book.

When I heard the door open I looked up to see Max step inside. He had a paper sack in one hand and his cell phone in the other.

"Absolutely you should come tonight. I can't wait for you to meet Sammy. We'll see you then." He hung up the phone and smiled as he walked toward me.

"We missed breakfast and it's almost time for lunch. I hope you don't mind that I just picked us up something."

"Great! I'm starving." I joined him at the table. "Was that your friend on the phone?"

"Yeah. Michelle's going to join us at the book signing tonight. She's a big fan of wine."

"Oh?" I smiled. "That's good. Did I tell you that Poppy warned me not to get drunk?"

"What a piece of work. I wish you didn't have to work with her."

41

"Actually, the more I think about it, I'm pretty sure working with her is going to be just what I need."

"What do you mean? She seems awful." Max frowned.

"I don't think she is. I think she's a bundle of anxiety and fear. I know what that's like."

"Maybe. So what are you going to do?"

"I'm going to introduce Poppy to some of the things that helped me along my way. I figure it will be a good reminder for me too."

"I don't know, Sammy." Max rubbed the back of his neck. "Do you think that she'll be open to it?"

"There's only one way to find out. If I don't try, I won't know."

"That's a good point. It's generous of you."

"One of the things I've learned is that if I'm bothered by something in someone else, it usually means I need to work on that issue myself. So, if Poppy's rigid behavior is bothering me, it's probably because I'm not as relaxed as I'd like to think. Doing this will be as much for me as it will be for her."

"Just remember, all of those rules and ideas are great, but some people are hard to get along with. Don't kill yourself trying to get her approval."

"Max, you know me too well."

"I should." He grinned. "And by the way, I hope you're keeping that outfit."

"Why?" I raised an eyebrow.

"Because I like it."

"Maybe we should get one for you then?"

"No."

"Why not, Max?" I grinned and leaned across the table to steal a fry from his plate. "I think you'd look great in it."

"No way." He narrowed his eyes.

"That's awfully unfair of you. You want me in something skimpy like that, but you won't wear it yourself."

"Trust me, what looks good on you, won't necessarily look good on me."

"Maybe not, but we won't know until you try!"

"Not going to happen, Samantha."

"Uh-oh, I'm in trouble now. You're calling me Samantha."

"Yes, you're in trouble." He stood up from the table and scowled in my direction.

I was a little startled by his expression.

"Max, I was just kidding. You're not upset, are you?"

"Maybe." He crossed his arms and settled his gaze on me. "How are you going to make it up to me?"

I rolled my eyes. "Oh, I see. We don't have time for that, Max."

"Oh no? We do. We have plenty of time. Poppy has everything scheduled perfectly, so I know for a fact that we have plenty of time."

I raised an eyebrow.

He raised one back at me.

"Alright, fine. But only for a little while."

"Great!" He grinned and tossed off his shirt, then sprawled across the bed.

I climbed onto the bed beside him and ran my hands along the curves of his shoulders.

"You're tense. What's going on?"

"I didn't like the way that Poppy's been speaking to you."

"It not a big deal."

"To me it is."

I frowned and decided to change the subject. "Tell me about Michelle."

His muscles grew tense again.

"What do you want to know?"

"Well, you said you were friends for one summer as kids, but that doesn't tell me much."

"I was twelve."

"Oh, boy—twelve." I grinned and rubbed his shoulders a little deeper. "I bet Michelle was your first crush."

He was silent as I ran my hands down along his back and worked on the muscles beneath his shoulder blades. Emotional knots could be just as difficult as physical knots to release, and sometimes it took work on both to get rid of either.

"Max? Did you fall asleep?"

"No, I'm awake."

"So? Was she your first crush?"

He turned over beneath me and looked up into my eyes. "You're not going to get weird about it, are you?"

"Of course not." I smiled and brushed his hair back from his forehead. "It's not as if I'm not aware of the thousands of women you dated before we got together."

"Thousands?" He furrowed an eyebrow.

"Millions?" I smirked.

"I think you overestimate my charm."

"So? Michelle?"

"Okay, okay."

I slid off him and he sat up.

"I'm just curious."

"If you must know, Michelle was my first kiss. But I'd rather you not mention that when we get together."

"Aw! I can see it now. Little Max, all nervous and shy." I kissed his cheek.

"I was twelve, not seven."

"Still." I gazed at him as I imagined the encounter. "Did she break your heart?"

"Not exactly."

"Oh boy, I shouldn't be surprised. You broke hers, hm?"

"No, it wasn't like that. We were just kids, it was one summer, and when I went back home, things ended."

"Oh." I studied him for a long moment. "So she's the one who got away?"

He met my eyes. "No. You're the one who got

away—until I caught you." He laughed and tackled me back down onto the bed. "Now let me return the favor of that massage."

I relaxed as Max rubbed my shoulders through my shirt, but my mind traveled in time back to that summer he'd spent with Michelle. First loves were hard to get over.

I couldn't help but wonder what it would be like for Max to see Michelle again.

CHAPTER 8

I dressed very carefully for the book signing. I didn't want to disappoint Poppy again. But I also made sure to add splashes of color and fun items, like a scarf and big bracelets.

When Max stepped out of the bathroom, I was surprised to see him in a suit.

"Oh, you're looking quite dapper."

"Dapper? What does that even mean?" Max flicked the lapel of his suit jacket. "I'm downright handsome."

"Well, that's true." I smiled as I looked him over. "I guess we're both trying to make a good impression tonight."

"I just want to look my best for you, babe." He kissed my cheek as he walked past me to the door. "Speaking of which, we'd better get going or we're going to be late."

"There should be a car downstairs for us." I grabbed my purse and my phone and followed him out the door.

On the way down the front steps I noticed a couple huddled close to the railing. I smiled to myself as they both put their hands on the carving.

"Isn't that sweet, Max?" I smiled. "We'll have to do that before we leave."

"Our relationship doesn't need luck, sweetheart. We have everything it could need—love."

I met his eyes as my heart filled with warmth. "That's for sure."

In the car on the way to the book signing Max gazed out the window.

"Do you remember any of this from your summer here?"

"Oh, London? No." He shook his head. "I stayed with relatives on a farm. I never went anywhere near London."

"Seems odd to be sent all the way to London just to end up on a farm."

"Well, it wasn't a pleasure trip. I'd been getting into some trouble and my mother thought a few months of hard work would straighten me out."

"Oops, that didn't work." I grinned.

"It did a little." He laughed. "I was still mischievous, but I did learn that I didn't want to end up becoming a farmer. Between the manure and getting up at the crack of dawn, I couldn't wait to get back to school and homework."

"I bet." I smiled as I studied his profile. Despite the fact that Max and I had been friends for so long, it fascinated me that there were still things I didn't know about him. Little things, like being exiled to a farm—and big things, like his first kiss. I wanted to know all of those things.

The car pulled to a stop in front of a small building. We stepped out and made our way to a thick red door. The gold handle was a bit garish against the old wood. I grabbed the handle and tugged it open. Right away piano music filled my senses. It was a light soothing melody that was akin to a breath of fresh air.

"Oh, Max, it's a piano bar." I looked at him with wide eyes. "Isn't this fantastic?"

"Yes, it is." He glanced up and down the sidewalk, then at his watch. "Let's go in."

As soon as I stepped through the door Poppy rushed toward me.

"Oh yes, this is much better." She looked over my off-white cotton dress. "It'll stand out against the black background of the stage too."

"I'm going to be on stage?"

"Oh yes, it's the best way for everyone to be able to hear you. Now remember Samantha, please be responsible about the amount of wine you drink."

"Poppy, I'm not a drinker—I promise." I looked into her eyes. "What about you? Are you going to have any wine tonight?"

"Maybe just a glass." She frowned and looked down at her watch. "We should get you on stage. The bartender is going to introduce the wines first, then you'll be the next to speak. Here is your copy of the book. I've highlighted the passage for you. Also, I tucked in some suggested responses to questions the audience might ask."

"I'm sorry, you wrote down my answers for me?" I raised an eyebrow. "Don't you think I should answer them myself?"

"Certainly don't say anything you don't agree with, but I think that you'll find the assortment of responses are fairly common."

"I'll definitely take a look." I gritted my teeth and reminded myself that this woman was suffering on the inside. Her need for control was really just a cry for help. I needed to stop thinking about what angered me and try to start thinking about how I could help Poppy.

I leaned close and kissed Max goodbye before I was led up to the stage.

CHAPTER 9

As Poppy adjusted the microphone and whispered a few last-minute rules, I noticed the door to the bar open and close. A woman walked in who held my attention. I didn't know if it was the dazzling gold dress, the perfect wavy blonde hair, or the lipstick so red that I could see it from the stage, but something told me that this woman was Michelle.

Max confirmed it when he walked over to her with open arms. She smiled so wide when she hugged him that I could practically count her teeth if I'd been so inclined. My nerves bristled the moment I saw them embrace.

Now, I'd seen Max hug many women. And sometimes—especially if I was feeling insecure about my looks—I did get jealous. But most of the time I was fine with it. This time I was not.

I gripped the microphone so tight that Poppy had to tug it hard to get it free of my hand.

"I told you that the bartender is introducing the wines first." She huffed. "Are you sure you're up to this,

Samantha?"

"Yes, I'll be fine." I couldn't look away from Max and Michelle.

The entire time the bartender was talking about the wine selection, my gaze remained locked to Max and Michelle. He lingered near her side, though I noticed that only their elbows touched. Other than the initial hug they'd shared, his hands hung by his sides.

I wanted to look away.

Remember, Sammy, you're his wife and there's nothing to be jealous about.

Maybe I could have looked away if she wasn't so beautiful. She wasn't rail thin—she wasn't even close to skinny. She was about my weight, give or take a few pounds.

So, was he attracted to her? Did he look at her and wonder what his life would have been like if he'd never returned to America? My heart lurched at the thought.

Was Michelle his path not taken?

"Samantha?" I blinked and looked over at the man who was holding out the microphone. From the stares of the audience I assumed that the bartender had tried more than once to get my attention.

"Thank you." I took the microphone from him and smiled as I stepped up to the edge of the stage.

Poppy cringed. She pointed to the podium, but I ignored the direction.

"I think we're all here tonight for one reason." I

looked around at the mostly female audience and smiled. "The wine!"

Laughter followed my comment.

I took a breath and willed myself to relax. This was an important moment, not just for me, but for my career. I couldn't let a little jealousy distract me.

"I've always said, the best thing to pair with a good glass of wine is a good book. On that note, I'd like to read a passage to you."

As I launched into the passage that Poppy had chosen, I learned a bit about her. The passage she'd selected was full of passion. It surprised me that she would feel a connection to that section of the book. I glanced up at her as I read.

Her usually passive expression came alive with a curve of her lips, a subtle dip of her lashes, and a flush in her cheeks. I smiled to myself as I spoke the last few words.

There was no question in my mind that Poppy had a hidden passionate side. I was going to break it out—right after I made sure that Michelle kept hers hidden.

I narrowed my eyes as I noticed the way she reached for Max's hand and offered him a glass of wine. She giggled when he sniffed at the glass—giggled!

"Here! You need some wine too!" One of the members of the audience leaned up to the stage with a full glass of wine.

The truth was, I really did need a glass of wine.

I leaned forward to grab the glass, but in that moment Michelle leaned close to Max's ear. I was just distracted enough to only grasp the edge of the glass. As I tried to catch it, my foot slid forward off the front of the stage. I lost my balance within an instant, but the tumble felt like an eternity.

As I fell, the wine splashed back into my face. I anticipated the crush of the floor as my body struck it. What I felt instead was the warm flexibility of palms under my shoulders, back, and backside. It was not at all what I expected to feel. I tried to open my eyes, but the wine stung when I did.

Aware that I was moving, I soon put together that the audience had caught me and I was being passed along from person to person. I blinked enough to clear the wine from my eyelashes and saw the stage before me. Someone beneath me gave me a solid shove and I ended up on my feet on the stage, right where I'd started.

My off-white dress was stained in dark red wine. It made me think of a horror movie, but it wasn't nearly as frightening as the look on Poppy's face when I looked over at her.

"Sorry, everyone, but I think it's pretty well-known that I will dive for wine."

The audience laughed again—all but Poppy, who stood with her arms crossed.

CHAPTER 10

I took a few questions and shared another glass of wine, then Poppy stepped up on stage to wrap up the event.

As I settled at a table to sign copies of my book, I looked over at Max and Michelle. Max's cheeks were a little pink. I knew that look—one too many glasses of wine.

Michelle's chair was very close to his. I couldn't see it, but it was quite possible that under the table their knees touched.

Luckily Poppy walked up to distract me.

"I never expected that, Samantha, even after everything I learned about you during our visit in Amsterdam."

I looked up at her. "What?"

"Stage diving?" She shook her head. "What if someone had gotten hurt? And look at your dress."

"Poppy, it was an accident. My foot slipped."

"Which never would have happened if you'd been

standing near the podium like I'd instructed you."

I signed a book for the last person in the line, then cleared my throat.

"Poppy, I like to be connected with my audience."

"Oh? Well, you certainly were tonight, weren't you?" She frowned.

I bit the tip of my tongue. I actually bit it. I didn't want to let loose the words that were building in my mind.

Instead, I smiled.

"It was an accident, but I have to say that I was pretty impressed that my fans caught me. It was a really fun experience and one that never would have happened if I'd played it safe and stayed behind the podium."

"Exactly my point." She rolled her eyes. "There's no need for antics like that."

"Haven't you ever made a mistake? Have you ever tripped or walked into something when you weren't looking?"

"Not really. I'm always pretty cautious. I keep an eye on everything around me and plan for what might go wrong."

"But you can't plan for everything. Like, you had no idea the night would end in crowd surfing."

"That's for sure." She sighed. "You prevent me from predicting what might go wrong."

"I know that probably makes you a little uneasy— actually very uneasy, I'm guessing. I understand that feeling. I'm not here to make your life harder, Poppy."

"You're not?" She frowned. "Because my life feels harder right now."

"Maybe what you're feeling is a desire to have a little chaos in your life."

"Why would I ever want chaos?"

"Because some of the most beautiful things are born out of an accident or a terrible situation. The unpredictable is often when miracles happen."

"That's a bit much, isn't it?" She scrunched up her nose.

"I don't think so." I turned and looked over my shoulder at Max. "See that man over there?"

"Your husband, yes." She smiled. "He seems like a nice guy."

"He's a very nice guy. And if I hadn't shaken up my life a little, he would not be my husband. I took a chance—let a little chaos in—and as a result, I'm now married to the man of my dreams, a man I never even thought I had a chance with. Sometimes a mess is the perfect way to discover what you really want. And sometimes making a mistake is the only way we'll end up on the path we're really looking for."

"I guess I've never thought of it that way. It just makes more sense to do what's expected—to make the right choices—avoiding the probability of mistakes."

"It does make sense, until you think about what you might be missing out on. So many people—including myself—just strive for perfection with a goal of being flawless. But, in my experience, it's the flaws that create life. It's the wrong turns and the embarrassing moments that teach us and help us grow into the people we really are."

"But it's so much simpler when things are all in the right order."

"I hear you." I picked up a glass of wine from the table and offered it to her. "But I have a feeling there's a part of your life that you wish was a little messy."

She took the glass and met my eyes. "Is it that obvious?"

"Only to me. Only because I've been there myself. There was a time when my world was as small as a laundromat and the customers in it. It felt safe that way. I was in control. But I took a step out of my comfort zone—several steps, in fact—and now look where I am." I smiled. "Sure, you don't have to go crowd surfing, but it might be time to admit that you're looking for romance."

"How did you know?" Her eyes widened.

"I see the way you look at Max."

"Oh, please. Don't think that I—"

"I don't." I picked up another glass of wine from the table. "I know it's not him you're longing for, it's the relationship. I've felt that way too—for far too long—trust me. So I hope you don't mind if I give you a little advice."

"I'm listening."

"The only way you're going to find that love of a lifetime is if you open your heart and your mind."

"I don't know if I can do that."

"If you let me, I can help." I held her gaze. "If you give me just one day, I promise you, you'll never be the same."

Poppy glanced away from me and sighed. "I don't doubt that. But what will I be like after?"

"I can't tell you that. The question is, do you want to spend the next five years exactly the same way, or do you want to shake things up a bit and see what happens?"

I looked over at Max.

He raised his glass of wine to me. "Sammy, come meet Michelle."

"I'll be right there." I smiled at him, then turned back to Poppy. "What do you say? Just one day. How much damage could I do?"

Poppy cringed. "I'd rather not think about it."

"Just leave it in my hands. I promise you won't regret it."

She managed a smile and a slight nod.

CHAPTER 11

As Poppy walked away I wondered if she would follow through with the agreement. I hoped that she would.

"Sammy." Max caught my hand with his and tugged me toward him. "This is Michelle. Michelle, meet Samantha."

"Hi, Michelle." I smiled at the woman before me. I tried not to notice how close she stood to Max. I didn't want to think about what my hair smelled like or what my dress looked like from the wine spill. "It's so nice to meet you."

"You too, Samantha. I've heard so much about you. Max doesn't ever stop talking about you." She laughed.

I smiled again and pretended not to be surprised that Max had spoken that much to her about anything.

"He's told me some things about you too. I hear you two had quite a summer together."

"Oh, he told you about that?" She laughed. "We thought we were in love, didn't we, Max?"

Max lowered his eyes as his cheeks flushed. "Just kids

being kids." He nodded.

"Well, I'd invite you for a drink, Samantha, but I think you've already had one." Michelle laughed.

I liked her laugh. I wanted to like her. But there was something in the way she looked at Max that made me very uncomfortable.

"Maybe another night? When I haven't already showered in wine."

"Good idea. It's late." Max wrapped an arm around my shoulders. "I know Poppy planned a big day for us tomorrow."

"Actually, I might want it to be just her and me, Max. Would you mind that?"

"Of course not. Whatever works for you."

"Oh, well, if you're not doing anything tomorrow, I could show you around the old neighborhood," Michelle directed toward Max.

"I don't know." Max shook his head. "It might be a bit far."

"You wouldn't mind would you, Sammy?"

There it was. She called me Sammy. Only Max called me Sammy—and maybe a handful of very close friends— but mostly just Max. I took a deep breath and forced a smile to my lips.

"It's fine with me. I'd rather Max have a fun day then be stuck at the Inn doing nothing. Just make sure you bring him back to me."

"I can't make any promises." Michelle laughed again.

I didn't like her laugh any more.

Max grinned. "Oh, wild horses couldn't keep me away." He kissed my cheek. "Mm, tasty." He kissed my cheek again. "We should get some of that wine to take home."

"Alright," Michelle said, "I'll leave you two to get some rest. Maximillion, I'll pick you up in the morning."

"Great." He squeezed my shoulder and pulled me closer.

When Michelle walked away I took another deep breath. My main focus was just to keep control of my feelings. There were a whole lot of them brewing and tempting me to say the wrong thing. Maximillion? Michelle's pet name for *my* husband?

"What a night, huh?" Max led me toward the door.

"It seems to me that I've had quite a bit of bad luck since arriving in London. I hope tomorrow will turn that around."

"You have something up your sleeve, hm?"

"Don't I always?" I grinned.

On the drive back to the Inn, Max looked over at me from the back seat of the car. "So what did you think of Michelle?"

I set my jaw and turned my attention to the window. I didn't want to let those feelings begin to brew again.

"I think she's beautiful and I think she seems to be very fond of you."

"Oh? Who wouldn't be?" Max elbowed me gently, grinning.

The car stopped in front of the Inn.

"Good point." I smiled as we stepped out of the car.

He slid his hand into mine. "You know you're the only one for me, right, Sammy?" He met my eyes.

I looked back into his. "Yes, I know."

Early the next morning I awoke to pounding on our door. It woke me from a dream about bathing in wine. It was lovely and a little strange at the same time. Bleary-eyed, I patted Max on the back of the head.

"Max, someone's at the door. Max." I cleared my throat.

Max groaned into his pillow.

All of a sudden I wondered if I'd forgotten to set my alarm. Was it Poppy outside, already irritated at my tardiness? I bolted upright in bed and looked at the clock. It was barely seven in the morning. I wasn't supposed to meet Poppy until eight-thirty. I still had fifteen minutes to sleep.

But the pounding continued on the door.

"Who could that be, Max?"

"Let me get it." He sighed and rolled out of bed.

He pulled on a pair of pajama pants over his boxers along the way. When he reached the door he leaned his forehead against it.

"Who's there?"

"It's me, Michelle."

I could hear her from where I lay still in bed.

"What?" I sat up in bed and yawned. "You guys are going out this early?"

"I didn't realize." Max frowned, then he called through the door. "Give me just a minute, Michelle." He turned back to face me. "Are you okay with this, Sammy?"

"Max, she's your friend." I climbed out of bed and grabbed a robe. "Invite her in for some breakfast."

"No, that's alright. You should be able to get a little more rest. I'll just meet her outside."

I took a breath as I watched him rush to get dressed. I noticed that he took a few extra strokes with his comb through his hair. He stared in the mirror a little longer than I'd expect him to. Or was I just imagining it? Was I hypersensitive to his need to look good for Michelle?

"Hey." I wrapped my arms around him from behind and leaned forward to kiss his cheek. "You look as handsome as ever."

"Thank you." He tilted his head back to give me a quick kiss.

I ruffled my hand through his hair and pulled him close for a longer one.

When he pulled away he smiled, then he picked up his comb and fixed his hair.

I took a deep breath and willed myself not to think terrible things. Max had never given me a reason not to trust him. It wasn't right for me to doubt him, I knew that. But watching that comb glide through his hair made me think that it was far too important to him to look his best for Michelle.

CHAPTER 12

I walked with Max to the door. When he opened it, I wished that I hadn't. Michelle stood outside in the cutest outfit. Her hair tumbled across her face in a sexy way. I glanced over at Max.

"Sorry about the wait. I guess I'm not used to getting up with the cows any more."

"I guess not." She smiled. "I figured if we got an early start we'd have plenty of time for me to show you some of the things that have changed. I think you'll be surprised. Of course, Samantha, if you get done early, you should join us."

"No, that's okay. You two have fun." I swallowed hard and looked away. Did she notice? Did he?

Max offered me a quick peck on the cheek and then headed out with Michelle at his side.

I closed the door and tried not to collapse. There had been moments in the past—especially before we were together—that I'd been jealous of the women Max dated.

But this was different. My husband, Max, had just left

with a gorgeous woman, who happened to be the first love of his life—and all I did was smile at them as they left.

Should I have put my foot down and stopped it from happening? Should Max have refused to be alone with her?

I sighed and closed my eyes. "I trust you, Max, I trust you, Max, I trust you, Max."

My cell phone alarm began to ring. I rushed over to it and turned it off just in time to see a text come through from Poppy.

I'm ready when you are.

I smiled. That brightened my mood. I had wondered if she might try to get out of our bucket list. I sent her a text back to meet me at a coffee shop in thirty minutes.

After a quick shower I dressed and headed out the door. My main focus was to keep myself as busy as possible. The less time I had to think about Max and Michelle alone together, the better.

On my way to the coffee shop, I thought about all the times Max had proven his love for me. Yet what stuck in my thoughts was how dismissive he'd been about the love story behind the carving on the railing at the Inn. Would he feel that way if things had worked out with Michelle?

Maybe he was so cynical because he'd never felt that kind of passion and desperation again. Maybe he felt that way because he could easily move on with his life without me if he had to.

The thought made me feel sick to my stomach. I pushed it out of my mind as I opened the door to the coffee shop. It was easy to see that, although it was a bit late for breakfast, the place was popular. Many of the tables were occupied.

Poppy waved to me from one of the tables.

"Hi." I smiled as I walked over to her. "Ready for our big adventure?"

"I said I'd give it a shot. I'm not promising more than that."

"Let's start it off right. I'll be right back."

I walked over to the coffee bar and ordered us two of the most expensive drinks topped with every sweet thing they had. When I carried the drinks back over to the table, Poppy looked up at me with a grim frown.

"I can't drink that. It's full of sugar."

"It's one morning, one treat." I pushed the drink toward her. "If we're going to start an adventure, it should always start off sweet."

"If you say so." Poppy sighed and took a sip of her coffee. "Mm. Okay, that is delicious."

"See? It's not just about the sugar. It's about the flavor. It's about the way it awakens all of your senses. Now you're more open to the idea that it could be a good day, right?"

"Maybe a little." She smiled.

"Great. Because it's going to be an amazing day. I

have it all planned out."

"Interesting." Poppy raised an eyebrow. "I thought the point of this was to be more spontaneous?"

"Spontaneity is fine when you have plenty of time, but we have a lot of ground to cover in a short time. So I've put together a bucket list of things for us to do today. But there's one very important thing that's missing."

"What's that?"

"Your big wish."

"My big wish?" She laughed. "What is this, some kind of fairy tale?"

"It could be, if we do it right. But it's important to have that one huge thing that you want deeply—but maybe don't really believe will happen—in the front of your mind. You'll be amazed at just how much closer you'll get to it, just by staying focused on it."

"I'm not sure that I have any big wishes, though. I mean, I pride myself on dreaming within my means. If it isn't realistic, I don't want it. Who wants to walk around with a longing for something that could never come true?"

"You think you have that kind of control over your desire, but if you're honest with yourself, I bet there might be a few big wishes that you've been ignoring."

"I pride myself on honesty too."

"Okay, but it's a lot easier to lie to yourself than it is to lie to anyone else. So let's see if we can't get to the bottom of this, hm?"

"How?"

"We can play a little game."

"Okay." She shrugged. "I'm already on a sugar high, why not play games too?"

I smiled. "It's not as childish as you might think. Just close your eyes."

"Here? In public? I'm not sure that I'm okay with that."

"Just give it a shot. It'll be better than you think."

"Okay, I'll try." She closed her eyes.

CHAPTER 13

Once I saw Poppy's face relax, I lowered my voice.

"Now just take a long slow breath. Not deep, not timed, just long and slow, as if you can taste the air that passes through your lungs."

I watched as her chest began to rise, then lower. "And one more slow steady breath just like that. Feel it nourish your body." After her next breath I lowered my voice even more. "Think of warmth—the kind that starts deep in your belly and connects to your heart. Think of how it swells up within you. It feels similar to being hugged, or finding a long-lost favorite item. Think of that warm feeling. Can you feel it?"

Poppy nodded, but didn't open her eyes or speak.

I studied her closely. "Now, one more slow and steady breath. When you breathe in, you feel that warmth building. As you breathe out, you'll remember just what makes you feel that way. It'll be a picture, a smell, a sound, or a feeling. Just let it form within your mind. When you're ready, open your eyes."

A moment later her eyes sprang open. "Wow."

"Is that a good wow?" I smiled.

"It's just a wow. That was pretty interesting."

"So? Did you see something?"

"Maybe."

"You don't have to tell me what it was, but more than likely, it's your one big wish. Do you think you could write it on a slip of paper? You could keep it with you. I'll never have to look at it. There's something concrete about writing things down. It's as if you can bring fantasy into reality."

"Yes, I can do that." She grabbed a napkin and took the pen I offered her. She jotted down a few words, then folded the napkin into a tiny little square. She tucked it safely inside her pocket.

"See, you do have a big wish."

"Maybe, but it doesn't change anything. It's never going to happen. Still, I do have to say that I feel a lot calmer than I did even a few minutes ago. You really made a difference there." She drank more of her coffee.

"Sometimes all it takes is slowing down a little. Most people don't take the time to realize the fast pace we keep with everything in our daily lives. Our minds, spirits, and bodies yearn for that slow purposeful breath. Did you know it's actually fairly common for people not to breathe enough? There are people who are so stressed that they often hold their breath."

"I can understand that. Life can be very demanding."

"Yes, it can be." I nodded and finished my coffee.

"But not today. Today we do things for the fun of it, not because we have to."

"Well, actually you're doing things for the fun of it. I'm doing things because you think I need to."

"Give it a little time and you're going to be having just as much fun as I am."

"I hope that's the case." Poppy stood up from the table. "I'm going to go wash up."

As soon as she was gone, I pulled out my phone. Just as I was about to text Max, he texted me a photograph. He had his arm around Michelle as they stood in front of an old farmhouse. It was a friendly gesture, I knew that. I typed back a quick message.

Have fun.

Then I swiped the picture out of view. As my heartbeat raced, I recognized my loss of control. Max had sent me a picture to show me some of his past, and I could barely look at it.

When Poppy returned to the table I stood up. "Let's head out."

"Now?"

"Yes, better to get moving." I smiled.

My phone buzzed with a text, but I ignored it.

I hailed a taxi and we drove to the gathering I'd selected to start our morning.

Poppy raised an eyebrow as we walked into a carpeted room filled with people sitting on the floor with their legs crossed.

"What is this?"

"You're going to love it. It's a great way to start things out. We'll be nice and relaxed when we're done." I gestured to a spot on the carpet. "There's a good place to sit."

"I'm not sure if I'm comfortable sitting on the floor."

"Just give it a shot. You might be more comfortable than you expect." I sat down and smiled up at her.

Poppy eased her way down to the floor.

I noticed the ultra-conservative shoes that she wore. Despite the fact that her outfit was put together well, she'd chosen very plain footwear. I assumed that she made most of her choices in life based on what made the most sense and not necessarily on what she wanted.

Once she was settled, I pointed to the front of the room. "See those white bowls?"

"Yes."

"They're called crystal singing bowls. I love to meditate to the sound of them."

"Ah, meditation. Yes, I've tried it. It doesn't work for me."

"No?" I raised an eyebrow. "I didn't think it would work for me at first either, but over time I learned how to relax. That's the key to meditation, at least it was for me—letting go of control."

"But don't you think it's kind of silly?" She frowned. "To sit in a room full of strangers with your eyes closed? I mean, anyone could do anything and you wouldn't even know it."

"I don't think anyone here is going to hurt me. Is that something that you worry about?"

She lowered her eyes and picked at the hem of her shirt. "I've had a bit of experience with being harmed."

"I'm sorry." I touched the back of her hand. "Maybe you use control to protect yourself?"

"I think it's necessary."

I nodded and looked up at the front of the room as the bowls began to sing. "I can understand that. But the thing about control is that it only gives you the illusion of protection. The truth is, there's no way to keep yourself safe all the time. Things happen, chaos explodes, and bad people walk into our lives through no fault of our own."

"Maybe. But there are some things that can be done to prevent some of that—like not closing your eyes in a room full of strangers."

"Okay." I smiled at her. "Fair enough. Keep your eyes open. But let the sound wash over you from head to toe. The vibrations may surprise you."

"Okay." She nodded.

CHAPTER 14

As the sounds grew louder I closed my eyes. I wanted the vibrations to eliminate the negative emotions that swirled within me. I wanted to discover my peace.

But with every new chime, my heartbeat quickened. I couldn't relax. The moment my thoughts drifted, the picture of Max with his arm around Michelle filled my mind. I had plenty of friends. I took pictures with their arms around my shoulders all the time. I tried to convince myself that my concern was over nothing.

After a few slow deep breaths, I was able to get my shoulders to relax. More than anything, I wanted my focus to be on Poppy and not let Max and Michelle's adventure distract me.

When I surfaced from my semi-meditation, I was pleased to see that Poppy had her eyes closed. Just when I thought she must have been comfortable enough to close her eyes, I heard a subtle snore escape her.

"Poppy?" I touched her shoulder gently.

She jumped and opened her eyes. "What?"

"I think you fell asleep."

"Oh." She rubbed her cheek and wiped away a bit of drool. "I guess I did. I've never had that happen to me before."

"Maybe the sounds relaxed you."

"I guess they did." She laughed. "You know it's funny, I actually feel pretty good. Like I just stepped out of a shower."

"That's good at least." I smiled. "I always enjoy spending a little time in meditation, especially if I have a very busy schedule to keep up with."

"I wonder if there's a way to get that in a pill form. Like, pop this pill, and you'll feel like you just meditated." She grinned. "I think I would like that."

"I might too." I laughed.

"Where to next?" She met my eyes.

I saw it then, the eagerness within her to embrace the experience. All of my concerns about Max and Michelle began to fade beneath my desire to introduce Poppy to a more relaxed and fulfilling lifestyle.

"Well, we needed that rest, because I've got us booked to participate in an adventure obstacle course."

"A what?"

"It's hard to explain until you see it."

"Or maybe you just don't want to tell me?" She raised an eyebrow.

"Maybe." I grinned.

The outdoor obstacle course was located in the

middle of a large park. The air was chilly, but the sky was clear and blue. It seemed like it would be a good day to experience some intense physical activity. Since my run hadn't gone so well the day before, I looked forward to getting some endorphins flowing.

"Oh, Samantha, what are you thinking?" Poppy stared up at the wooden wall that towered before us.

"I'm thinking it's just one more obstacle that we can easily get through."

"If you think I'm climbing over that, you've lost your mind!"

"The only way past is over it." I smiled at her. "This is how we learn just how strong we are."

"I'm not that strong." She shook her head. "Besides, look at what we're wearing."

"They have jumpsuits, don't worry."

"I'm not worried, because I'm not going to do it. I could get hurt, then I'd be out of work. Why would I risk that?"

"Listen, a lot of things could happen. But if you're always taking the safe path, then you're going to miss out on a great deal of life. If you really don't want to do this, then fine, we'll move on to the next item on the list. But I can promise you that the sense of freedom and accomplishment you'll experience is something you'll never have the opportunity to experience behind a desk or in the safety of your home. If there's one thing I'm certain of about you, Poppy, it's that you enjoy a challenge."

"How do you know that?"

"If you didn't, you wouldn't have invited me to London."

She sighed. "I guess you're right about that."

"So let's get up and over that wall. Hm?"

"Alright, I'll try it."

After we were outfitted in jumpsuits we approached the wall. There was a rope for Poppy and a rope for me. Excitement pumped through me. Poppy had agreed to try, that meant a lot. But the moment I grabbed the rope, it struck me that it meant I had to try also. I gave the rope a hard tug. It seemed solid enough.

The scuff of shoes against wood drew my attention to Poppy. Already she'd gotten a few feet off the ground.

"Great job, Poppy!"

"You next!" She panted.

I took a deep breath. This was something that I needed more than I'd realized.

I climbed the face of the wall with steady movements. Poppy matched my pace and we shouted support to one another. Everything about our climb up was going well, but I realized that getting over the top of the wall was going to be much harder. Although I got one of my legs swung over, heaving the remainder of my weight when my muscles were exhausted from the climb was difficult.

It struck me that I was quite out of shape. Not that I'd been an athlete prior to the book tour, but I'd at least built up some stamina. All of that seemed to be gone now.

"I think I'm going to fall, Samantha!" Poppy clung to the top of the wall.

Her leg did look like it might slip back over the front of the wall.

"You can do it, Poppy. Just push your leg a little higher. You can do it. See?" I pushed harder until I was fully straddling the top of the wall.

Poppy grunted and shoved her leg further over the top. A moment later she was straddling the wall as well.

"You did it!" I smiled.

"Right, but we still have to get down there." Poppy pointed down the other side of the wall.

Somehow, on the way up, it didn't seem as high as it did looking down from the top.

"Easy!" I managed a grin. "I'll race you!"

"Wait, Samantha, you should be careful—"

CHAPTER 15

Poppy's words echoed in my ears as my foot slid along the front of the wall. There was no traction, but in my attempt at enthusiasm, I'd swung both legs over without thought to getting a foothold. The rope burned my palms as I slid all the way down the wall and landed hard on the ground.

"Samantha?" Poppy screeched. She bounced her way down the front of the wall as if she'd been scaling walls for years. "Are you okay?" She crouched down beside me as one of the rangers ran up to me.

"Are you injured?" He placed a hand on my shoulder.

"No, I'm okay. Just embarrassed."

"It happens all the time. Just remember, safety first. Think about your next step before you take it."

"See?" Poppy smiled and offered me her hand. "A little caution goes a long way."

"You're right." I laughed as I stood up. "Maybe I should slow down just a little bit."

"What do you mean, slow down? We're done, aren't we?"

"Well, there's still that." I pointed to a low balance beam that snaked across a swamp-like pond.

"Are you kidding me?" She shook her head. "I can't do that."

"That's what you said about the wall, remember?" I winked at her. "I don't think I believe in your *I can't* any more."

"This is different."

"It's not. The only reason that you think you can't do it is because you haven't tried. But if you give it a shot, I bet you can."

"Or I'll end up in slime." She scrunched up her nose.

"It's pretty shallow, ladies, you'll be fine." The ranger winked at Poppy.

Poppy's cheeks grew red right away.

I raised an eyebrow and smiled to myself. First her longing look at Max, now an instant blush the moment a man spoke to her. I had a feeling I knew what Poppy's big wish was.

"Maybe you could show us how it's done, ranger?" I smiled at him.

"Oh." He pulled his hat off. "I'm in more of a supervisory role."

"See, I don't think my friend Poppy is going to do it, unless she sees that it's safe." I lifted an eyebrow. "I'm sure that she'd feel a lot better if she knew that you could cross it."

"Is that right, Poppy?" He met her eyes.

"I just—well, I don't think." She lowered her eyes and shrugged.

He smiled and put his hat back on his head. "Just for you, Poppy. Keep an eye on me, alright? I haven't done this in a while."

"I will." She smiled at him. It was a tiny awkward smile that made my heart burst with warmth.

"Sir, what's your name? So we can cheer?" I stepped forward before he could mount the balance beam.

"Robert." He nodded to us both, then began to make his way across the low board.

"Why did you make him do that?" Poppy frowned.

"Why not?" I smiled. "He's a handsome man in action. Don't you think?"

"I didn't notice." She flushed.

"Sure you did." I elbowed her. "I think he likes you."

"Why would you think that? He barely looked at me."

"No, you barely looked at him. He looked at you the whole time."

"You're making that up." She rolled her eyes and looked back at the ranger. "Wow, look. He's almost across."

"Let's give him some support. Go, Robert! Go, Robert!" I waved my fist above my head.

"Samantha!"

"Try it." I smiled at her.

"I'll feel ridiculous."

"So?"

"Go, Robert!" She raised her voice just a little.

Robert stopped on the balance beam and turned back to wave to her. As he did, he slid right into the water.

"Oh no! Look what happened! Samantha, this is all your fault!"

Poppy's face was red and I could see her stress level rising right before my eyes.

"What? I didn't do anything!"

I rushed forward as Robert floundered in the water, but before I could reach him, Poppy shot across the balance beam to Robert's side. She reached down and stretched out her hand to him.

"Here, let me help you."

"Thanks, Poppy. Be careful." He grabbed her hand and eased his way back up onto the balance beam. "Thank you so much."

"Please don't thank me. I'm the one that made you fall."

"No, you didn't." He offered a sheepish smile. "I fell because I was trying to impress you."

"What? Why?" Poppy stumbled back and nearly lost her footing on the other side of the balance beam. Robert grabbed her and pulled her close.

"Careful now. Let's get to the other side together." He took her hand and began to lead her toward the other side of the beam.

I made my way to the other side and stole glances back at the two. By the time they'd crossed the beam, their hands were interlocked.

"Fantastic! You made it." I grinned.

"And you cheated." Poppy huffed and put her hands on her hips.

"I was only trying to help."

"Don't worry, Poppy came to my rescue." Robert smiled at her. "I hope you both enjoy the rest of your adventure."

I saw the disappointment in Poppy's expression as he walked away. "You should ask him for his number."

"What? No." She shook her head. "I couldn't do that."

"Sure you could. Just go do it."

"Enough." She laughed. "You're not going to get me to do that."

"Alright, alright. Maybe it's time we get some lunch."

"After all of that, yes, I'm ready to eat."

"I'm going to stop in the restroom and I'll meet you out front."

"Okay, I'll call for a taxi."

CHAPTER 16

I was almost to the restroom when Robert walked up to me. "You're not doing the whole course?"

"No, I just wanted to give Poppy a taste. We have a lot of other things we have to do this afternoon."

"I see." He cleared his throat and glanced over his shoulder. "Is she still here?"

"Yes, she's waiting out front for me."

"Oh." He nodded and rocked back on his heels. "She seemed like a nice person."

"She is." I smiled and met his eyes. "Just shy."

"Hm. I gathered that." He glanced over his shoulder again, then back at me. "This will probably seem incredibly forward and inappropriate, but I'm going to take a chance. Would you mind giving her my number?" He held out a small piece of paper. "I'd ask her myself, but I don't want to put her on the spot. If she wants to call she can, if she doesn't, it's fine."

I smiled as I took the piece of paper. "I'll make sure that she gets it."

"Thanks." He tipped his hat as he walked away.

91

I thought back to that moment when Poppy had thrown all caution aside and rushed to his rescue. It was a beautiful example of just what kind of person she was.

When I met up with her at the front of the park she turned to face me.

"What took you so long?"

"Oh sorry, I just got caught up." I kept the note in my pocket. I wanted to give it to her at the end of the day, after she'd had the chance to complete the adventure.

I instructed the driver to drop us off beside a group of shops.

Poppy stepped out with a frown. "I thought we were going to lunch?"

"Before we can make our lunch reservation, there's somewhere we have to be."

"Let me guess—a shark cage?" Poppy laughed.

"Now there's an idea." I grinned. "That would certainly be outside of my comfort zone."

"Mine too." Poppy fell into step beside me. "So where are we going?"

"Well, if we're going to eat at a fancy restaurant, then we need something special to mark the occasion." I paused in front of a small shop that featured several extravagant hats in the window.

"How exactly is a hat going to mark the occasion?"

"Come inside." I opened the door and invited her to step in front of me. Once we were inside I closed the door.

The shop was even better than it had looked online. The walls were lined with hats covered in feathers, animals, and even replicas of famous buildings. There were so many that I had to crane my neck to see them all. "We're going to buy new hats to wear to dinner."

"What?" Poppy took a step back and shook her head. "Samantha, these are fun to look at and everything, but there's no way I could ever be seen in one of these." She clutched her purse tight in her hands.

"Why not?" I looked from her white knuckles to her wide eyes. "Obviously people wear them or there wouldn't be a shop. Why can't we wear them?"

"Because." She frowned and looked down at her conservative shoes. "People will notice. People will stare."

I smiled and brushed a hand along the curve of her shoulder. "I know what it's like to want to hide, Poppy. It's so much easier to go unnoticed—to be the invisible person in the room. But that's not what I really wanted. I wanted to be noticed. I was just afraid that if I was, I would be judged."

"Wearing a hat like that—I would be." She pointed to a hat that consisted of a high heel and a leg from ankle to thigh. "I mean, what would people think?"

"That's it exactly." I smiled and picked up a hat that featured a monkey on a tree branch with a bunch of bananas. "We base our lives around fear of what other people will think—around that judgment. It becomes such a deep-rooted anxiety that we can't ever do anything to draw attention to ourselves. But the whole point of this activity is to experience what it's like to have that attention. What does it matter if someone stares? Does it really do any harm? What does it matter what other people think? Are they really going to have any influence on your life?"

"I don't know." Poppy frowned and looked at my hat. "I don't think I'm ready for something like this."

"Well maybe not like this." I lifted the monkey off my head. "The point isn't to just draw attention for the sake of drawing attention, but to present a part of yourself that you would normally keep hidden. If you can find a hat that expresses a passion, a secret desire of some kind, that is the kind of hat that we will wear to dinner. So take your time and look around at all the options. I'm sure that we can come up with something that will work."

Poppy shuffled through hat after hat. The entire time the note burned in my pocket. Should I give it to her? Should I wait? Should I tell her what a good impression she'd made on Robert? It was hard to decide. On the one hand, it wasn't my place to keep it from her. On the other, I knew revealing it too soon might distract her from our goal for the day.

CHAPTER 17

"I think I found something." Poppy smiled as she picked up a hat that was decorated with stars, moons, and planets. She ran a fingertip along a sprig of golden stars.

"It's beautiful. But does it mean something to you?" I studied the hat.

"It does." She nodded. "The truth is, I've always been fascinated by astronomy. When I was a little girl I wanted to be involved in space any way I could. But as I got older, I started to see that it wasn't a realistic career option. My parents pointed out that I'd be much better off getting a degree and owning a business than trying to break into a field like that." She sighed and gazed at the crescent moons that covered the black felt of the hat. "But I still spend a half hour every night looking up at the sky—even if it's cloudy, even if it's raining. I look, because I know it's all still out there, whether I see it or not."

"That's such a beautiful way to spend a half hour, Poppy. I never would have guessed that you had that interest. That's a hidden part of yourself, but the question is, why are you hiding it?"

"Because it still hurts a little when I think about it. A part of me, I guess, wishes that I had gone after my dream instead of settling for the career path that made sense. Maybe I wouldn't have been smart enough. Maybe I wouldn't have been able to find a job. But at least I would have tried."

"Yes." I nodded. "That's how I felt about writing at one time. I thought I could never be a real writer. I could never be published, or achieve any kind of success. It was just a passion of mine, not a career choice. But when I allowed myself to take that chance, look what happened." I smiled. "There's always time, Poppy, to answer that quiet call inside of you—to embrace your true passion."

"Is there?" Poppy picked up the hat and placed it on the top of her head. "I think that time has passed for me."

I reached up and fluttered the sprig of stars so that they caught the light in the shop and twinkled. "It's only passed if you let it be a memory instead of a desire."

"You seem so confident." Poppy sighed. "I don't think I could ever do the things that you've done."

"Really?" I stared into her eyes. "I have no doubt that you can."

"What makes you think so?" She bit into her bottom lip.

"You're a strong woman, Poppy. I see that in the way

that you maintain everything in your life in a perfect schedule. You always have your eyes wide open to the world around you and you care that things go just as you plan them."

"I thought you said that was controlling?"

"It is." I smiled at her. "But that doesn't make it wrong. It just shows how much control you can truly have over your life. Right now that control is directed at pleasing others, or meeting the expectations that you believe are expected of you. What if you turned all that strength and all that energy into a direction that benefited your true passion?"

"You mean going back to school?"

"Why not?" I shrugged. "There's plenty of time to do just that. Or perhaps you could align your choice of work to be more related to astronomy. There are many ways to get to your passion, you just have to be open to it. Right now, you've told yourself your dream is dead, that it was ridiculous to dream of it in the first place. You're looking back at the young girl who knew exactly what she wanted and telling her that she had no clue how to be Poppy— that her instincts and desires were wrong."

"I never considered that." She shook her head slowly, which caused the stars to dance. "It's rather harsh when you put it that way."

"It's very harsh, Poppy. That's the point. We are trained to trample down our true selves for the sake of the comfort of others. But what about that quiet voice inside of you that still calls you to the sky each night? It might be muffled by the stress of day-to-day obligations, but it's still there, it's still waiting to be heard."

She blinked to hide the tears in her eyes. "All of this from a hat?"

"And we haven't even bought it yet." I smiled. "So will you wear it?"

"Yes. Yes, I think I will. But what about your hat?"

I glanced around at the shelves. The truth was, I was as confused as Poppy. My true desire was once to become a writer and then to be with Max. What was left for me to want?

My eyes settled on a hat that featured an assortment of paths. Each one was different. Some were brick, some were dark soil, some were white sand. But all of the paths intertwined and wrapped around the hat to lead back to the same small house on the top of the hat. It was a small cottage, nothing too fancy. But to me, it was home.

I picked up the hat and put it on my head. Then I turned back to Poppy and smiled. "What do you think?"

"I think you are homesick." She smiled and looked into my eyes. "I never really thought about how hard all of this travel might be on you."

"I don't think that's quite it. The thing is, Max and I got married and then launched into this tour so fast. It's almost as if we didn't have a chance to put down our roots, to create our home." I rubbed the brim of the hat and tugged it down a bit. "I guess I'm longing for that place to call home, that sense of family."

"And maybe that?" She pointed to the hat.

"What?" I took the hat off my head and saw that she'd pointed at a tiny replica of a swing in the front yard of the cottage.

My eyes widened. Was that it? Was I longing for a child? The very thought shocked me. There were times in life when I'd wanted a child and times in life when I was happy not having one. Had that desire surfaced without me even realizing it?

"Maybe. I'm not sure."

"Will you wear it to lunch?" She grinned.

"Yes, I think I will. Let's go check out. It's almost our reservation time."

Despite the fact that Poppy fought me most of the time we were in the shop, she purchased her hat with a gleeful smile. She even wore it right out of the shop.

I adjusted my hat as I stepped out behind her. A part of me wished I could hide that swing. For some reason, I felt the need to hide the possibility that I might want to have a child. Why was it that I felt some shame about it?

CHAPTER 18

I didn't have much time to think about it. When we arrived at the restaurant, Poppy opened the door, then turned around and walked the other way.

"Wait, Poppy—what's wrong?" I grabbed her hand.

"Remember how you asked me whether I thought anyone who saw me in this hat would have any influence on my life?"

"Yes." I glanced toward the window of the restaurant.

"Well, there's someone in that restaurant who could have a very big influence in my life. At least, I hope he might."

"All the more reason to wear it, Poppy." I held her gaze. "This isn't the time to disappear again."

"Please, Samantha, I don't even think he knows that I'm alive. If this is the first time he notices me, he'll think I'm some kind of nut."

"Or maybe he'll think that you're a creative, fun woman who has an affinity for space." I stroked her hand in an attempt to reassure her. "This didn't happen for no reason, Poppy. What are the chances that this man would be at the restaurant where we're going to eat on this very day? There's more at work then an accidental encounter. If you walk away now, you'll have never tried, just like you never tried to go after your dream."

"Oh, Samantha, this is too hard. I'll look so silly."

"I'll be there with you." I reached up and pushed the tiny swing on the top of my hat. "You won't be the only one getting stared at. Just try it for a few minutes, and if it's really bad, we'll get up and leave."

"I don't know." She clutched her purse tight again. "It is strange that he just happened to be here, isn't it?"

"Strange or perfect?" I smiled. "Which do you think is more likely?"

"What does it matter?" She groaned. "I look ridiculous."

"You look wonderful. Let's just go in and see what happens. Can we?"

"Yes, I guess." She sighed. "I've come this far, haven't I?"

I held the door open for her.

As soon as we were inside I regretted coaxing her into it. The man she was focused on sat at a table near the kitchen and across from him was a woman. It wasn't just any woman, but the kind that took the breath away of anyone that looked in her direction. She had her hand wrapped around his as they spoke in intimate tones.

"Oh. I guess he's not single." She sat down at the table and closed her eyes. "I'm such a fool."

"You're not a fool." I sat down across from her. "So he's with someone right now; that doesn't mean he always will be."

"It's not just that. It's foolish of me to have even thought about him having an interest in me. He was in my shop the other day and I recognized him from the magazines I stock the stand with. He's some multi-millionaire or something. Anyway, I guess I thought we had a moment as I rang up his purchases. We chatted about books, and he stayed longer than he needed to. In my head, I built up this whole fantasy that we would meet again one day."

"There's nothing foolish about that. If it's what you want, that's what you should go after."

"Obviously, he has a bit different taste in women. It was silly of me to even consider it. I guess I'm just getting a little lonely. At least I have you to share lunch with."

I noticed the sadness in her gaze. I'd led her into the lion's den and now she was crushed. A fancy hat wasn't going to fix that, but I knew something that might.

I pulled out my cell phone and hid it on my knee under the table, then I pulled out the folded-up note. I texted Robert with the address of the restaurant and asked him to join us. Poppy didn't notice. She was too busy perusing the menu.

A minute later I received a text in return.

Would love to meet up. Be there soon.

I looked across the table at Poppy and wondered if

I'd overstepped. I'd never really had the chance to play matchmaker before. I hoped it wouldn't blow up in my face.

"You know, sometimes we can be so focused on what we think we want that we don't even notice what it is that we really want."

"What do you mean? I really want a salad and that's what I'm going to have."

"That's not exactly what I'm talking about." I laughed. "I mean, like Robert today."

"Robert? The ranger?"

"Yes."

"What about him?"

"He was handsome, wasn't he? You two shared a moment."

"Sure. But he wouldn't be interested in me." She shrugged.

"What makes you think that?"

"I don't know. I'm not the adventurous type."

"You were today."

She sighed and looked over at the man and his date. "Can I admit something to you?"

"Yes, anything. I'm listening."

"That man over there—he's my big dream. He's what I wrote down on that napkin."

My heart sank. "Oh wow, Poppy. I didn't realize. I'm sorry if I've put you in an awkward position."

"No, it's okay. I needed to see this. I needed to face

some reality. I guess I'm just getting tired of being alone. Valentine's Day makes it harder."

"I remember what that was like." I sat back in my chair. "Every holiday can be tough when you're longing for someone to share it with."

"That's just the thing. Most of the time, I can ignore it. I keep myself busy with work and everything else. But when I slow down, that's when it hits me that everyone is pairing up, except for me."

"That can change at any minute."

"I don't know; as routine as my life is, there isn't much room to meet someone."

"But you did today." I bit into my bottom lip and glanced toward the large windows of the restaurant. "And he asked me to give you his number."

"What?"

"Robert gave me his number to give to you."

"Really? Oh, I could never call him!"

"You don't have to. I invited him to lunch." I stood up from the table as the door swung open.

Poppy looked up at me with wide eyes.

"Your big dream wasn't a name on a piece of paper, it's a person to connect with. Maybe it will turn out to be Robert. You won't know unless you try."

Poppy paled as Robert walked up to the table. "I hope I'm not interrupting."

"Not at all, I was just leaving." I winked at Poppy and headed out of the restaurant, fearing just a little that

Poppy could end up being very angry with me the next time I saw her.

CHAPTER 19

I spent the rest of my afternoon exploring London. I tried to push the thought of Max and Michelle out of my mind.

Though I missed Max, it was actually nice to experience some of London on my own. I took lots of pictures to share with him, and the thought of having something new to share with him was pleasant. Since we lived, worked, and traveled together, it wasn't often that I had the chance to share my experiences with him after the fact.

As I perused some of the shops, I thought about what I might want to get Max for Valentine's Day. He was difficult to buy for. With his logical mind, any overly romantic gifts always fell flat. He seemed to prefer practical things.

This year, I wanted it to be different. Just like Poppy and I had found hats that represented our desires, I wanted to find something that would represent Max's desires. But the more I searched, the more lost I felt. Did

I even know what Max was passionate about? Could someone really be passionate about computers and technology? Maybe.

I fiddled with a few pendants of computer monitors and keyboards, but that just seemed silly to me. I wondered what Max might truly want—what he hoped for in the future. The more I wondered, the more it bothered me that I didn't know these things right off the top of my head.

Would Michelle know? I sighed and shoved the thought down.

In the past—before we'd begun dating—I would have said that Max's passion was spontaneity, never being held down, always free to explore his desires. But now that he was married, where did all of that passion go?

I picked up a silver ring that had wings etched into it. Something about the sight of it saddened me. Had I clipped Max's wings? I set the ring down and looked through a few more items.

In the next few shops I looked at shirts, magazines, books, jewelry, and even video games. Nothing spoke to me of Max. I didn't want to just buy him something, I wanted to buy him the right thing.

It occurred to me that since we were in London where he'd spent some of his youth, maybe I should purchase him something that honored that. I noticed a pendant on a thin silver chain. The pendant was in the shape of a tractor. I pictured giving him the necklace and the strange look I would receive. No, Max was not a farmer. I sighed as my frustration built.

Just as I was about to give up, I stopped in an eccentric shop that featured crystal balls and evil eyes. It was really just on a whim that I peeked at the jewelry under the glass countertop. The moment I saw it, I knew it was what I wanted.

The pendant was a winged dragon. The wings were outstretched and the head was raised as if prepared to take flight. Maybe I couldn't figure out what Max's passion was, but I did know that it was there. Maybe this would remind us both that it needed to take flight.

I purchased the necklace with some relief and some doubt. Would he even like it? Would he think it was a bit childish? I had no idea.

When I returned to the room, it surprised me that Max wasn't there. Minutes turned into hours. I thought for sure he'd be back in time for dinner, but dinner came and went with no sign of him. I could have texted him, but that seemed a bit desperate to me.

So instead, I filled my mind with all the things that could be happening between him and Michelle. I sat on the edge of the bed and curled my hands around the hem of the comforter. There was no reason for me to be upset. I continued to repeat the words like a meditation mantra, but the words refused to sink in.

The more I thought it, the more upset I became. Another minute ticked by. Another breath left my lungs.

Another image of Michelle and Max curled up together in a barn somewhere flashed through my mind.

With a jolt I stood up from the bed. I needed to find a way to distract myself. I picked up my book and started to look through the pages, but the words blurred. I looked at the clock again.

When I drew another breath I hoped that I could calm myself down before Max walked through the door. The last thing I wanted was to pounce on him with an over-the-top accusation.

When I heard the door handle turn, my heart jumped into my throat.

CHAPTER 20

Max stepped inside and closed the door behind him. "Sammy, I didn't expect you to be home."

"You didn't?" I raised an eyebrow. "Where else would I be this late?"

"I just thought you must be busy with Poppy. I mean, you didn't text me all afternoon."

"You didn't text me either."

He walked toward me to kiss me, but I turned my cheek instead. "I didn't want to interrupt." He frowned and looked into my eyes. "What's wrong?"

"Nothing." I pulled away from him and sat down on the edge of the bed. "Did you have a good day?"

"It was nice." He nodded and smiled a little. "It was good to see Michelle again."

"I bet." I grimaced as soon as I'd spoken. The words just flew out of my mouth as if spoken by someone else entirely.

"Sammy." Max grabbed my hands and gave them a light squeeze. "You told me that you were fine with this."

"I am. I was. I don't know." I closed my eyes. "I'm sorry."

"Just tell me what's going on." He pulled me a little closer. "Are you upset with me?"

"I don't know what I am." I opened my eyes and sighed. "I don't know what's going on in my head or my heart. I know it's not your fault."

"That doesn't tell me anything. Is it Michelle? Sammy, you know we're only friends, right? And if it really bothers you, I don't have to see her again while we're here."

"I can't ask you to do that. You're old friends. I know it's not her fault either."

"Then what's going on? Sammy?" He paused a moment. "Can you look at me?"

I looked up at him as he requested, but regretted it the moment that I did. When I saw the hurt in his eyes, I knew I'd created it.

"I'm so sorry, Max. I keep trying to ignore these feelings, but they keep coming up."

"Then there's a reason for them. If I've made you feel insecure, I'm sorry."

"You haven't." I shook my head. "You've been very open with me. I guess it's just hard for me to think of you with your first love."

"Ah, Sammy." He sighed, then looked into my eyes. "You're my only love. Don't you know that?"

"I do. That's why none of this makes sense."

"Why don't we just sleep on it?" He hugged me and kissed my cheek. "If in the morning you're still worried, then we don't have to see Michelle again."

"Max, I don't want that—"

"I'm not discussing it. You're the most important person in the world to me, Sammy, and if it makes you uncomfortable that I spend time with Michelle, I'm not going to do it."

"Like you said, let's just sleep on it. I'm sure I'm just worn out from my exhausting day."

"Did it go well?" He stretched out on the bed and patted the bed beside him.

"Better than I expected." I nestled in beside him and reveled in the warmth of his arm around me. When I closed my eyes, I didn't have a slew of fears race through my mind. Instead, all I knew was peace. Was I really so needy that Max had to physically be in the same room with me for me to trust him? I opened my eyes and looked into his. "I love you, Max."

"I love you too, Sammy." He kissed my forehead, then closed his eyes.

I watched him for some time as he rested, and wondered what thoughts might be on his mind. Did he think about our future? Did he ever consider the family we might have? Just when I thought I might be brave enough to ask him, he snored.

I laughed as quietly as I could and sprawled out beside him. Maybe the time wasn't right to bring it up.

Maybe all of the chaos inside me was more about what I wanted from my own future instead of what we might share. The book tour was great, but it wouldn't last forever. What would come next?

The next day Max and I toured a lot of the same places that I'd checked out the day before. I kept to myself the fact that I'd already seen most of it. He was his usual loving self, stealing kisses and hugs whenever he could.

As the day progressed, I worried less about Michelle and thought more about the book signing that night. I took a moment at lunch to text Poppy.

How are you today?

A second later she texted me back.

Why did I think I could pull off something like this? What if no one shows up? Who even thinks of something like this? No one is going to get on stage and recite poetry!

I smiled as I texted her back.

It's going to be wonderful. Plenty of people will show up. It's a brilliant idea. I can't wait to be part of it. Make sure you invite Robert.

"Who are you texting?" Max grinned as he leaned over my shoulder to take a peek.

"Poppy. She's freaking out about tonight."

"Really? I thought she always had everything planned out to perfection."

"I guess it doesn't matter how planned it is." I

glanced down at my phone as she texted me again.

Do you really think I should? What if he thinks I'm stalking him? We had a nice time at dinner, but that doesn't mean we're anything more than friends. Does it?

I shook my head as I remembered how on edge I had been whenever I wondered if a man truly wanted to date me. It was a terrible feeling.

Trust me, he wants to be more than friends. Invite him.

CHAPTER 21

I put down my phone after sending the text and looked into Max's eyes. "So have you heard from Michelle today?"

"Yes, she texted me earlier."

"Did you invite her to the signing tonight?"

"No. I thought maybe that wouldn't be a good idea."

"Max, I told you I was okay with it."

"I know you did, but I still think it wouldn't be a good idea. I'm looking forward to being there with you. I missed you yesterday."

"I missed you too."

He looked at my phone for a moment. "What's that picture of?" He pointed to a picture I'd taken the day before.

I realized in that moment that I'd been caught in a lie.

"Oh, uh—I did some exploring yesterday."

"I thought you were busy with Poppy all afternoon?"

"I was—until lunch."

"Why didn't you call me? You could have joined me and Michelle."

"I thought you two should have some time together."

"Sammy, I don't need time with another woman. She's just a friend and could be your friend too—if you'd let her."

"Max, I just didn't want to interrupt."

"Hm." He ran his finger across my phone to look at the other pictures. "So instead, you've been lying to me all day? Why?" He frowned.

"I just didn't want to mention that I'd already seen some of these places. I didn't want to ruin our day together."

He sat back in his chair and narrowed his eyes. "Lying to me kind of does that, don't you think?"

"Max, please." I rolled my eyes. "It wasn't a real lie."

"Seriously?" He laughed. "I didn't know there were fake ones."

"I mean, it's not like I was hiding something. I just didn't mention it."

"Alright." He reached out and took my hand. "But you were hiding something. You were hiding the fact that you didn't want to spend time with me and Michelle and also the fact that you've already been to half the places we've gone to today."

"So?" I shrugged. "What's the big deal?" I searched his eyes for an explanation.

"It's not a big deal—at least not that part. The part where you feel the need to lie to me at all is the big deal."

"Max, you're making too much out of this."

"I don't think I am." He shook his head.

"You are." I stood up from the table. "We'd better head back so that I can change for tonight."

"Sammy?" He caught my hand again and met my eyes.

"Yes?" I smiled at him.

"You can tell me anything, you know—anything."

"I know." I kissed his cheek.

We walked back to the Inn with silence between us. It was unusual. I liked to chat, he liked to tease. Quiet wasn't our typical thing. But I didn't know what to say. How could I explain what I felt about Michelle without insulting him or revealing that I might not trust him as much as I should? With Valentine's Day the next day, I didn't want to cause a fight.

Luckily, when we reached the Inn, there was a crowd there to distract us.

Max laughed at the long line of people that waited to touch the engraved initials.

"Look at these people. They really believe in all this."

"What's so wrong with it?" I shrugged. "Any little bit of luck when it comes to romance can be a very good thing."

"Real romance doesn't need luck." He shook his head.

"You don't think so?" I looked over at him.

"I mean, if you care about someone, then you care about them. It's not about luck, it's about chemistry and getting along. Right?" He smiled and kissed my cheek. "Chemistry and communication, baby, that's all we need."

"Don't you think it's a little more than that too? Like maybe fate plays a part in bringing the right people together?"

"I don't know." He led me through the crowd on the steps. "I'm not sure if I really believe in all that."

"All of what?" I paused at the top of the steps.

"That one true love nonsense." He frowned.

My breath left my body so fast that it was audible. Had he really just said that to me? It's not as if I didn't have that opinion myself at one time. But how could Max believe that? Did he think we just fit together well enough to get married? Was there truly no passion behind our marriage?

"Max, you don't mean that, do you?"

"What? It's too noisy out here. Let's go inside." He pulled me toward him just as a police officer rushed up the steps.

"Hey! None of that!" The officer pointed at a man bent over the railing as he attempted to carve something into it. "This is not your property!"

Max laughed again and steered me into the Inn.

The entire time we were in our room I wanted to bring up the topic again, but the truth was, I was a little afraid to hear the answer. What I really wanted was for Max to have a different answer. But was that just me being prideful? I wanted to be his one and only, and if he didn't truly believe that was possible, could he still be interested in someone else?

There wasn't much time to dwell on the disturbing thoughts I was now having. I had to rush to change and get ready for the book signing.

By the time we left, it felt awkward to bring it up again. I decided to let it go for the night and focus on the book signing.

CHAPTER 22

When we arrived at the bookstore, Poppy greeted me with a tight smile.

"Everything's fine, that's what I keep telling myself."

"Did something go wrong?" I met her eyes.

"Not really. I just haven't heard back from Robert." She bit her lip. "I guess maybe I shouldn't have invited him."

"I'm sure he's just too busy to get back to you right now. Try not to worry about it, Poppy."

"I'll try." She glanced at her watch. "Oops, time to get up there and introduce you. Are you ready for this?"

"I think so." I smiled.

"I know so." Max kissed my cheek and then gave me a hug. "Good luck, you'll do great."

"Thanks, Max." I kissed him back, then followed after Poppy as she headed to the small stage in the back of the shop.

She walked up to the microphone with a wide smile.

"Hello, everyone, and welcome to our speed dating poetry slam. Now you may wonder how we came up with this idea. Since I knew we'd have the honor of hosting a great writer so close to Valentine's Day, I wanted to come up with a way to mesh the idea of creative writing with the idea of romance. Perhaps it doesn't happen so often any more, but romance has a long tradition of being intertwined with poetry.

"So this evening each of you will have an opportunity to mingle, then if you'd like to come to the microphone and offer your own brief overture to the date of your choice, you can. At the end of the evening, our judges will select a winner of the poetry contest and that winner will receive a fully paid fantasy date for Valentine's Day. To get those creative juices flowing, Samantha is going to read us a passage from her book. Samantha?" She smiled and applauded as I approached from across the stage.

"Thank you, Poppy. I think this is the best idea I've come across in a long time. Words can really convey love and affection. When you think about it, everything we say can be a bit like a poem—when we're speaking from our hearts to those we care about. I hope this passage can give you some inspiration for your own poetry."

As I read the passage, I noticed that the people in the audience seemed to already be connecting. Many spoke in quiet tones to one another. Some just held hands, while others' eyes met across the room. The next day was Valentine's Day and the bookstore was buzzing with anticipation for it.

I looked for Max and spotted him seated in the back

of the room. He toyed with his phone while I finished the passage. As applause filled the room I noticed he didn't clap. It wasn't as if he had to. He went to every single one of my book signings. This was routine for him. But the fact that he didn't bother to look up from his phone made me wonder just who he might be talking to. Was it Michelle?

The thought made my voice catch in my throat. I waved to the audience instead of speaking and walked over to the judges' table. Music filled the shop. People had the opportunity to move from table to table in an attempt to get to know as many people as possible. Every time the buzzer went off, those at the tables switched.

I smiled to myself as I remembered my own attempt at speed dating. A sense of relief anchored itself within me as I realized that I'd never have to do that again. I would never have to worry about being alone on a holiday again. Even if Max and I were apart for some reason, we wouldn't be alone.

As the night continued, I noticed a latecomer. Poppy noticed him too and waved to Robert as he approached her. I watched as the two smiled at one another and exchanged nervous small talk. It was beautiful.

The buzzer sounded again and Poppy walked up to the microphone.

"Alright, everyone, that's it for the speed dating portion of the evening. I truly hope you found someone that you connected with. Remember, finding love means taking a risk." She looked over at me and winked, then she turned back to the audience and continued. "Now, no one is required to come up here and recite poetry. But if you want a chance at winning the heart of someone you connected with, or a chance at winning the all-expenses-paid perfect Valentine's Day date, then you have one hour to come up here and give it a shot. Thanks, everyone!"

She walked away from the microphone.

I looked over at Max. He still had his phone in his hands.

One by one people walked up to the microphone to speak their short poems. Most of them were men, but a few of the women braved the stage as well. The poems were short and sweet, but nothing that really held my attention.

Maybe that was because Max held it. A small part of me wished he'd storm the stage and recite a poem for me. Sure, we weren't participating in the competition, but here was a chance for him to show his passion for me, and he couldn't be bothered to barely glance up from his phone.

Just as the event was winding down, a woman stepped up onto the stage. Her eyes remained trained on the floor. Her hair fell in her face. Her clothes hung loose around her body as if perhaps she was attempting to hide it by wearing a size that was too large. With hesitant steps she walked up to the microphone.

CHAPTER 23

My heart softened for this woman. Clearly, she was very shy.

She cleared her throat and the microphone screeched.

"Oh, I'm sorry. I'm so sorry." She sighed. "I never do things like this. But I want to take a chance tonight."

I looked around at the audience to see if there were any men looking in her direction. I didn't notice anyone in particular.

"Let's hear it!" I smiled and clapped my hands to encourage her.

She jumped at the sound.

"Okay, okay." She took another deep breath. "Maybe. Maybe you saw something in me. The way I saw something in you. Maybe something could be blossoming between you and me. It's so easy to walk away. It's so easy to wait until another day. It's so much harder to look you in the eye and hope that it's worth a try. I like the way you laugh and that your favorite animal is a giraffe. I like that you touched my hand and told me that my shyness is something you understand. I like that you took a moment to get to know me and make me think that you might really see—that maybe I could blossom for you. Maybe what I felt is something that you feel too. Maybe you could take a chance on me." She gripped the microphone stand tightly.

My heart ached for her. It was the emotion she conveyed through her words—the hope, the hesitation, the preparation for rejection—that reminded me so much of myself.

My heart swelled as I searched the audience for anyone that she might have been directing her poem toward.

Just as she started to walk away from the microphone, a man stood up and approached the stage. He held out his hand to her and helped her as she made her way down the steps.

The audience went wild with applause. I couldn't stop smiling. All the judges at the table shared a few words and nodded. She was the clear winner, but before we could announce it, Poppy took the stage.

"Hello again, everyone. I want to say that this has been a wonderful event. Although I'm obviously not competing for the prize, I would like to say a few words to someone special." She looked over at Robert, who grinned and blushed at the same time. "I'm no poet, but I just want you to know that I will always come to your rescue, just like you've come to mine."

Robert stood up and plucked the rose out of the vase on his table. He walked over to Poppy and held out the rose. "We might not be able to win the contest, but I've won something much more valuable." He offered his hand to her and she stepped down from the stage.

After the applause faded, I took her place at the microphone to announce the winner of the poetry contest. It meant more to me to see the light in the shy woman's eyes than the entire event. In that moment her life had changed, and I was very familiar with that feeling.

I lingered for just a few minutes more at the microphone and looked across the room at Max. I thought about making my own declaration of love for him, but he was still gazing down at his phone. My lips tightened.

I turned away from the microphone as the event came to an end. By the time I'd walked off the stage Max was waiting for me at the bottom of the steps. He wrapped his arms around me and kissed my cheek.

"That was fun." He smiled.

"Was it?" I shrugged. "You looked busy."

"I was." He sighed. "I'm sorry. I hoped that you wouldn't notice. I know it was rude of me, but Michelle was having a crisis and I just wanted to be there for her."

"A crisis?"

"She's asked me not to mention it to anyone." He held my eyes. "I'm sure that you can understand that."

"I do." I took a deep breath and silenced my rioting

mind. "I absolutely do." I kissed him and then took a moment to gaze into his eyes.

Maybe Michelle did need a friend, and that was okay. Max's arms were still around me, and with Valentine's Day the next day, I was sure that Michelle wouldn't even cross either of our minds.

Early the next morning Max woke me up with a kiss. I stirred and smiled at him. This was it. This was my Valentine's Day gift—to be able to look into his eyes the moment I woke up every morning.

"I love you, Max."

"I love you too. Happy Valentine's Day." He kissed me again.

We lingered in the bed for some time before he finally tugged me out of it.

"I have a surprise planned for you."

"Max—"

"I know, I know, you don't like surprises. I think you'll like this one. Wear something comfortable, okay?"

"Okay." I smiled and picked out my outfit.

When Max was in the shower, I tucked his present into my purse. My heart skipped a beat as I wondered where we might be going.

By the time we were in the car together, my mind buzzed with all the possibilities. London had plenty to offer when it came to romance. However, it wasn't long before I realized that the car Max had hired for us was headed out of the city.

"Where are we going?"

"It's a surprise."

"Okay." I smiled and nestled my hand into his.

Glad that we'd put the tension behind us, I relaxed into the anticipation of what Max might have planned. My mind drifted to Poppy and Robert, who'd shared their first Valentine's Day together. There was so much pressure at the beginning of a relationship to get things just right. Max and I were past that stage, which I found to be quite a relief. I did feel slightly anxious about the gift I'd selected for Max, though. It was just a token, but it had sentimental value and for some reason I really needed for him to appreciate that.

CHAPTER 24

We drove for over an hour. When the car turned down a long dirt road I started to get a little concerned about Max's plans.

"Where are we, Max?"

He looked over at me and smiled. "I thought you might like to see where I spent my summer."

"Your summer with Michelle?"

He raised an eyebrow. "There was more to it than that, you know."

"Oh." I forced a smile to my lips, but inwardly my mind churned. Why would he bring me to a place that would remind him of an old girlfriend? I pushed the thought away.

He opened the door for me and led me down a narrow dirt road to an old farmhouse.

"No one's living here at the moment." He wrapped his hand around mine. "Look at that sky." He smiled and leaned his head back to look up at the expansive sky above us.

For an instant, I forgot all about my sour mood and

lost myself in the same sky that he did.

Then he gave my hand a squeeze. "I know that you were feeling a little left out. I thought, what better way to fix that, than to give you a tour of this part of my life?"

"It's wonderful, Max." I tried not to think about the fact that this was the same place where he'd shared his first kiss with Michelle. I tried not to picture them chasing each other around, full of childish dreams and passion. It was silly, to be so caught up in the past, a past that didn't even belong to me. "Show me everything."

He pulled a key from under the front mat and unlocked the door to the farmhouse. As he led me through the rooms and shared little stories about the time he'd spent there, I sensed how much the place meant to him.

Enraptured by his memories, I held his hand tight in my own.

"Thank you for showing me this, Max. I had no idea that this time in your life was so important to you."

"To be honest with you, it changed everything, Sammy. During that time, I'd been so focused on being a rebel, I could have ended up in jail or worse. My grandfather knocked that right out of me and taught me how to value what mattered. Without my summer here, I'm not sure that I'd be who I am today."

My chest tightened. Without his grandfather or without Michelle?

"I love who you are today, Max. I'm so glad that you

shared this with me."

"There's more." He tugged me toward a clearing.

I saw a table set out in the middle of the lush green grass. The white linen tablecloth whipped in the wind. Tall candlesticks stretched toward the sky and two plates piled with food awaited us.

"Max? How did you manage this? It's amazing." He pulled out my chair for me. As I sat down, he leaned close.

"I wanted this to be a special day for us. So I enlisted a little help."

"Help?" I met his eyes as he sat down across from me.

"Michelle. She set everything up for me."

"She's here?" I glanced around.

"No, she left about five minutes before we got here. Don't you like it? I know that you've mentioned a few times that I'm not always romantic. When Michelle suggested this, I thought you would like it."

"Who am I spending Valentine's Day with, you or Michelle?" I muttered the words under my breath.

"Hm?" He smiled at me.

"Nothing. It's great, Max. Thank you." I reached into my purse. "I'm not sure if you're going to like this or not, but when I saw it, I thought of you." I handed him his gift.

"I have something for you too." He smiled and fished a small present out of his bag.

"Oh, but all of this is more than enough."

"No it's not, Sammy." He held my gaze. "It's never enough." He pushed the gift toward me.

I smiled and waited for him to open his.

"Wow, this is an awesome dragon." He held it up in the light to look at it. "I couldn't have picked a better pendant."

"Really?" I smiled. "I didn't think you even liked dragons."

"I do. I really like the wings on this one." He slid the necklace over his head and smiled. "Thanks. Now open yours."

I unwrapped the gift and found a small ring box inside. I flipped open the lid to discover a delicate ring with a sunflower on the top of the band.

"Wow, Max, it's beautiful." I met his eyes across the table. "Thank you so much."

"I can't take all the credit. Michelle helped me pick it out. When I mentioned how much you enjoyed meditation she pointed out that sunflowers are a symbol of spirituality."

Every word, after he'd mentioned her name again, flew right past me. So Michelle had even picked out my Valentine's Day gift? That meant that Max and Michelle had been browsing through rows of romantic gifts and jewelry.

"Sammy? Aren't you going to try it on?"

"Oh yes, of course." I slid it over my finger. It was a

perfect fit. "Oops, it's just a little loose. I'm going to keep it in my purse for now. I'd hate to lose it here."

"Good idea." He nodded. "I'm sure we can get it sized. If you like it."

"I love it." I leaned across the table and kissed him.

"And I love you." He stared into my eyes. "I'm so lucky that I get to spend the rest of my life with you, Sammy."

My heart softened and warmth flowed through me. There he was—my Max, the man who loved me.

CHAPTER 25

After we finished our lunch, Max led me down a winding path to a small pond. When we paused beside it, I could see the way his entire body relaxed.

"Was this your place to retreat when you lived here?"

"Yes. I used to come down here and skip stones."

I pictured young Max picking out the perfect stone. It was nice to get to know him in a deeper way. I leaned against a nearby tree and watched as he lingered close to the water. When I brushed my hand across a wide branch, I felt something unexpected. When I moved my hand I saw that there were initials carved into the branch—M and M. My breath caught in my throat. There was no question in my mind that the letters represented Max and Michelle.

"Want to try?" Max held out a stone to me.

My mind spun. Had they been here together just like this? Was it crazy of me to be jealous of a love that had taken place so long ago?

"Sure." I took the stone from him. When I tried to fling it across the water it broke the surface and sank right in.

"Here, let me help you. It's all in the wrist." He wrapped his arm around my waist and trailed his hand down along my wrist. "You have to flick it, like this." As the stone skipped, my heart did too.

Was it more foolish to doubt Max or to remain blind to a romance that clearly had never actually ended?

On the drive back to the Inn, I could only stare out the window. Max tried to coax me into conversation, but I couldn't offer anything more than one-word responses. Michelle cooked my Valentine's Day meal, Michelle picked out my gift, Michelle was part of Max's life long before I'd come into the picture.

When we arrived at the Inn there was still a small crowd of people that were waiting to gain some luck from the railing. What I thought was sweet, even magical just a few days before, I now saw through jaded eyes.

I managed to get through the rest of the evening with the best attitude I could muster, but long after Max was sound asleep, I was still wide awake. I stared at the ceiling and waited for that familiar warmth to fill me—the feeling that usually came just from being close to Max.

Instead, I experienced a sensation of emptiness. I buried my nose up against the curve of his neck and breathed in the scent of him. What should give me comfort only reminded me of what I would miss. Would he lose interest? Would he recall what it was like to carve those initials into the tree branch during a summer that was probably the hardest of his life?

When the sun peeked through the curtains, I was still wide awake.

Max yawned as he woke up. "You're up early."

"Mm-hm." I nodded.

"I forgot to mention yesterday that I invited Michelle to dinner tonight. I hope that you're up for it."

"Sure, anything for Michelle."

He reached for me, but I climbed out of bed before he could get a hold of me.

"Sammy? You alright?"

"Just feeling a little off. I'm going to take a nice long shower."

"Are we going exploring again?"

"I don't know. We could just stay in, I guess."

"We're in London, Sammy. Are you feeling sick?"

"Let me just get my shower."

As soon as I stepped under the hot water, my senses awakened. So did my common sense.

I was pulling away from Max when he'd given me no real reason to do that. His vows had been genuine on the day we were married. I knew that, and it wasn't right for me to doubt him.

When I stepped out of the shower, I found Max waiting for me.

"Max!" I jumped back at the sight of him and almost slipped on the wet shower floor.

He caught me by the elbow and helped me out.

"Still shying away from me, really?" He smiled and handed me a towel.

"I'm just a little out of it." I sighed. "I can't seem to get my head together, Max." I wrapped the towel around me. "I just feel like I'm backsliding. When I was with Poppy, it was great. It was like I was learning everything all over again. But then all of this stuff just seems to be cropping up. I just can't help but wonder when I'm going to get to the end."

Max brushed my wet hair back from my forehead. "Does it ever end really? I mean, we're in constant flux. So how does it end?"

"Ugh, I'd rather not think about that."

"Sammy, we used to talk about everything."

"Used to?"

"Lately, it seems you're giving me the brush-off. I'm not sure what's going on, but I hope that you know I'm here to listen. Anything that's bothering you, I want to know about it."

"I'm trying to figure it out. I think maybe the long break we'll have in Ireland will be good for me—good for us."

"Good." He kissed me.

It was the softest sweetest kiss. But my heart was still heavy. Somehow, I needed to lighten it up.

"You know what, I do want to go out today. Just give me a little time to get ready."

"Sure, I'll meet you downstairs when you're ready.

I'm going to check out the situation down there and see if we can actually get out the door."

"Okay, I'll be there in a few minutes."

As I pulled on fresh clothes, I also did my best to pull on a fresh attitude. If I couldn't get a grip on my emotions, then I would fake it until I made it. I would push myself to find the joy in every little thing—especially Max—until all of the unfounded worry subsided. It was a moment, it wasn't a lifetime. It was a tough time that I could overcome if I focused on everything positive in my life with Max.

CHAPTER 26

I met Max at the top of the steps.

"Not much of a crowd today, hm?"

"I guess with Valentine's Day over, no one's looking for luck any more."

"Maybe some people still are." I smiled. As I walked down the steps with him I brushed my fingertips along the carving. It certainly couldn't hurt.

The day was a blur as I pulled Max from place to place without giving either of us time to think or talk.

"Sammy, please, can we take a break?" Max laughed. "I don't think I can handle another museum."

"But we still have an hour before dinner."

"So, maybe we can just take a stroll together? Have a chance to speak to one another?"

"We've been talking all day."

"Not exactly." He slipped his arm through mine. "I need a little down time. Okay?"

"Okay. Look, let's walk past the shops, though. I'd like to take a peek in the windows."

"Anything not to look at me?"

"Max, stop!" I laughed and gave him what I thought was a playful shove.

Maybe there was more power behind the movement than I expected, because Max stumbled backward, catching the side of his leg against the edge of a fountain. In the span of a second, he went from being just behind me, to splashing into the fountain.

"Oh, Max, I'm so sorry!" I reached for his hand. "I didn't mean to do that. You have to believe me."

"You didn't?" He stared at me and grabbed my hand. "Are you sure about that?"

"Of course I'm sure. Here, let me help you." I started to pull him up out of the water.

"No, let me help you." He tugged hard and pulled me right into the water with him.

In the middle of a busy square in London the two of us were now splashing at one another.

"Max! What are you doing?"

"I'm giving us what we need!" He sent a wave of water in my direction. "It's time we had a little fun."

I was shocked and soaked and not sure whether to be annoyed or elated. When he sent another wave at me, I had to send one back. By the time we sloshed out of the fountain we were both soaked from head to toe.

"You said a stroll, not a swim!" I laughed as I dripped beside him.

"Hey, you pushed me first."

"Not that hard. You fell in on purpose, didn't you?"

"Maybe." He smiled at me. "I'm sorry, Sammy. I just wanted to break the tension."

"What tension?" My eyes widened. Had he felt it despite the fact that I'd tried to hide it all day?

He looked into my eyes for a long moment, then tilted his head toward the street. "We should get back to the Inn and change for dinner. I don't want to be late."

"No, we shouldn't keep Michelle waiting."

He studied me a moment longer, then slipped his hand in mine. "You're right, we should hurry."

When we arrived at the restaurant, Michelle was waiting out front. She waved to us as we walked up.

I did my best to put on a friendly smile.

"Hi, Michelle. Sorry we're a little late."

"Not at all, I just got here early." She grinned at me. "I'm sorry, I just feel like I want to hug you. Would that be okay?"

"Uh, okay." I opened my arms to her.

She hugged me and I returned the embrace with an awkward squeeze.

"I know we don't know each other that well, but Max never stops talking about you. I feel like I know you. Plus I read your book."

"Oh, you did?" I smiled.

"Yes, it's great. I really enjoyed it. I have to admit that I'm a little star-struck."

"Star-struck?" I glanced at Max.

Max grinned and shrugged.

"Your book is really popular with my friends and now with me too."

"I'm glad to hear it. I'll let you know when the next one is ready."

"Great, I can't wait."

"We should head in." Max held the door open for us. "Don't want to lose our spot."

Even with all of Michelle's compliments, it was hard for me to hold a conversation with her. My mind wandered to every look she seemed to be giving Max— every light laugh, every memory they seemed to share.

After we'd eaten, she excused herself to use the restroom.

The moment she was gone, Max turned in his chair to face me.

"Sammy, this has to stop."

"What?" I raised an eyebrow.

"You know what." He sighed and rubbed his hand across his forehead. "I told you before, if seeing Michelle is a problem, we don't have to do it. You just have to be honest with me."

"It's not a problem. Did I say something wrong?"

"You don't have to say anything, I can feel it."

I opened my mouth to tell him that he was wrong, but I couldn't bring myself to do it. The truth was, his instincts were right. "I'm trying, Max."

"If I can feel it, then I'm sure Michelle can too. I'm

not asking you to be best friends with her, but I would prefer it if you treated her nicely." He frowned. "I don't know what there is not to like about her. She reminds me so much of you."

CHAPTER 27

Max's words struck my heart like spears. If Michelle was so much like me, then what was he doing with me instead of her? Did he fall in love with me because I reminded him of her? Did he try to replace her with me? My heart raced.

"I'll try harder." The words felt forced out of my mouth.

He clenched his jaw and looked away from me. When he looked back, I could see the tension in his knitted brow. "This isn't like you, Sammy. Not at all. I don't understand it. Is it being here in London? Is it because you didn't like my plans for Valentine's Day?"

"I did like it." I bit into my bottom lip. Even though it was clear that my emotions impacted him in a hurtful way, I couldn't get them under control. "It isn't about anything, Max. There's nothing wrong."

He sighed and ran a hand back through his hair. When he spoke again, it was in a tone I hadn't heard him use in some time.

"There's something very wrong if you're lying to me

and keeping things from me, Sammy. I don't understand why you seem to think I'm blind to your feelings, or that I don't know you well enough to see that something is off."

My heart fluttered at the thought of confessing everything to him. Did I really want to reveal that jealousy had overtaken my rational mind to the point that I already had Max married off to Michelle with three kids and a field full of cows? What would he think of me then?

"I'm just going to use the restroom." I stood up from the table and did my best to ignore the way that his gaze followed me as I did so. Max did have his moments when he seemed to be able to peer right into the depths of me.

As I made my way back to the restroom, I coached myself.

You need to calm down, you need to get control of these feelings. Max doesn't deserve this. He's a good man, a trustworthy man, and you have no reason to doubt him. Get a hold of yourself Sammy!

I paused outside the door of the restroom and resolved to apologize to Michelle, or at least be more friendly to her. Just as I was about to push open the door of the restroom, I heard her voice, followed by laughter.

"You have no idea. I thought I was going to melt right then and there. I had no idea that he could kiss like that. If I did, I would have been demanding it from the start. Too bad it took so long for us to share it." She laughed again. "No way, I'm not sharing him. He's all mine. I just can't wait until everyone knows it."

My heart dropped. Max was all hers? She couldn't

wait to tell everyone? I narrowed my eyes and listened close.

"It doesn't have to be a secret much longer. It was such a relief to be able to tell him the truth after all these years. Anybody who doesn't like it is just going to have to get over it, because nothing is going to stop us this time. I let him go once and it's not happening again. That kiss told me everything I needed to know."

Tears filled my eyes at the thought of the passionate kiss that Max and Michelle had shared. Never did I expect my marriage to turn out like this.

I backed away from the door. My cheeks burned hot and my chest heaved with the sobs that I was desperate to hold back. My mind spun in a panic as I raced toward the door of the restaurant.

"Sammy?" Max stood up from the table as I rushed past him and out the door. I didn't wait to see if he would chase after me. What would be the point? He'd only end up telling me the truth—that he'd rekindled things with Michelle—and soon everyone would know it.

Alone in London, I had no idea where to go. After I'd run far enough away from the restaurant, I pulled out my cell phone and dialed Poppy's number.

"Hello?"

"Poppy, it's me, Samantha. Are you busy?"

"Just having dinner with Robert."

"Oh, okay. Never mind." I tried to hide my sniffle.

"Samantha, are you okay?"

"Yes, I'm okay." I swallowed hard and forced my emotions down. I didn't want to ruin Poppy's night with my problems. I also didn't want to be reminded that she and Robert were at that priceless part of the relationship where they were full of passion. "I just wanted to thank you again for everything."

"You're welcome. But are you sure that you're okay?"

"I'm fine. I'm sure." I hung up the phone and began to walk toward the Inn.

What would I say to Max when I saw him? A part of me wished he would continue to lie to me—just for a little bit longer. It hurt too much to think of those words coming out of his mouth.

"I'm sorry, Sammy, I didn't expect this to happen. I would never want to hurt you. I hope that we can still be friends."

I clutched at my stomach as it churned with revulsion. The life I'd planned now belonged to someone else. How could I ever be okay with that?

For over an hour I wandered, surrounded by strangers.

Max called me a dozen times but I didn't answer. Then out of the blue I heard his voice.

CHAPTER 28

"Sammy!" Max was jogging across the street toward me.

I thought about running again, but that would be ridiculous. I kept my eyes to the ground as he stopped in front of me.

"Why did you take off? Do you have any idea what you've just put me through?"

I stole a glance up at him. His red cheeks and swollen eyes told me all I needed to know. "I didn't mean to scare you."

"How would you disappearing in the middle of a foreign city not scare me?" He narrowed his eyes. "If I hadn't been able to track your cell phone, I would have called the police. I thought somebody took you. I thought there couldn't be any other explanation, because the Sammy I know would never just leave me behind like that, not even answering your phone to tell me that you're okay."

"I'm sorry." I tried not to look into his eyes. I didn't

want to think about the kiss he'd shared with Michelle. My heart broke every time I did. "I just want to go home, Max. I just want to leave."

"We can go back to the Inn right now—"

"No, I mean home." I reached up and wiped at my eyes before fresh tears could fall. "I want all of this to be over."

Max stared at me. "You don't mean that. This is your career we're talking about."

"I don't care." I shook my head. To my surprise, my words were true. I didn't care about any of it. If I didn't have Max, I didn't see how I was ever going to move forward with my life. There would be no recovering from his loss. "I'm done."

"What happened, Sammy?" He stroked his hands down my arms and tried to meet my eyes. "Tell me. I won't be upset. Just talk to me."

In that moment I should have told him what I'd heard. It was my chance to hear his side of the story. But I couldn't. I couldn't bring myself to speak the words that would end our marriage. I wanted to stick my head as deep into the sand as I could.

"It's just too much."

"We'll be in Ireland soon, Sammy. It'll be a nice long visit. We'll have plenty of time to rest up."

I sniffled and nodded. "You're right." I opened my arms to him. I just wanted to be held by him again. Maybe it wasn't healthy to still want his love after he'd betrayed me, but I couldn't imagine his arms never wrapping around me again.

He pulled me close and held me snugly against him.

"We'll figure it out, Sammy. Whatever it is. We'll figure it out together."

I wanted to believe him, but I wasn't sure if I even believed in anything any more.

Over the next few days I tried to find the perfect moment to mention the kiss. Max made sure that I didn't see Michelle again. He prodded me with questions, but I ignored them. I tried to focus on the next leg of the book tour—Ireland. It was a place I'd always wanted to visit but never dreamed I would make it to.

That was all good and exciting, but when the lights were turned out at night, Michelle's voice rang through my mind as I'd heard her describing the kiss. My world imploded—again and again and again.

On the day we were scheduled to leave for Ireland, Max stepped in front of me the moment I got out of bed.

"So it's been three days of this." Max paused in front of me and met my eyes. "I've been letting it go, because I know you're dealing with a lot of things, but I don't want to let it go so long that it doesn't get discussed." He folded his arms across his chest. "Out with it. I can take it—whatever it is."

I searched his eyes for any sign of a change. If a man kissed another woman, shouldn't there be some kind of rash? Some kind of telltale sign? A big C for cheater in the pupil or a splash of shadow on his skin?

"Did you kiss her? Michelle?" I blurted the question out along with every ounce of breath in my lungs.

"What?" His eyes widened.

For just a moment I thought he might lose his temper as his cheeks reddened. But he set his jaw and clenched his hands at his sides for a moment before taking a deep breath. I watched as his hands relaxed and his shoulders dropped.

"Is that what you think?"

"She was your first kiss, she was your first love—it's okay, Max. I understand. If it was just a kiss for nostalgia's sake, I'm okay with it—we can move past it. But if it was more than that, if you still have feelings for her—"

He cupped my cheeks and looked into my eyes. "I didn't kiss her."

"But I heard Michelle say that the kiss was amazing." I curled my hands around his wrists and held on to him. All of the fear that had built within me over the last few days bubbled to the surface.

I wanted to believe him, but I was terrified of what would happen if he chose Michelle over me.

CHAPTER 29

"I met her fiancée." Max narrowed his eyes. "I don't know what you overheard, but the only kiss that happened was between Michelle and her fiancée. I did help make that happen. Her family doesn't approve of him. They were meeting in secret at the old farm. When I found out, I gave her advice you've given to me and to your readers. I convinced her to take the next step and prepare to tell her family. I provided an alibi for her so that she could be with him."

"Oh." My heart slowed. Relief flooded through my body in cool waves. Everything Max was saying fit together like a perfect puzzle. If only I'd been able to see the whole picture from the beginning, maybe I would have thought twice before accusing him.

"Oh?" He let his hands fall from my cheeks and curl around my fingers instead. "That's all you have to say?"

"I'm sorry." I frowned.

The hurt etched itself across his features in the crease of his brow and the tension of his lips.

159

"You don't need to apologize." He spoke in such a quiet tone that I didn't know what to expect.

"Max, are you upset?"

"Shouldn't I be?" He shook his head. "I didn't expect this."

"I got a little crazy. I know that. I can't figure out why."

"Neither can I." He pulled me a little closer and met my eyes. "But obviously I haven't been showing you enough just how important you are to me. If you could even consider that I would do something to hurt you—"

"I know that, Max, I do. It's not you, it's me. I just—I don't know. I can't make sense of it."

"At least tell me the truth." He held my gaze. "Don't dance around it. This didn't come from nowhere. So what have I said or done that made you think that I would ever even think of kissing another woman?"

"You didn't do anything." I sighed.

"No, I'm not buying that. Something is off between us, Sammy, and I respect your right to personal space and your own emotions, but this isn't just about you. This is about us and our relationship. So why does Michelle, a woman I barely ever see, threaten you so much?"

"Because she was your first, Max. Your first kiss, your first love, and I just—" I cleared my throat and looked down at the floor. "I just wondered if maybe you felt more passion for her than you do for me."

"We were kids, Sammy."

"I know that." I frowned. "But you said you weren't sure that you believed in the notion of a one true love. I thought maybe that was because you'd lost yours way back then."

"Sammy." He hugged me and stroked a hand through my hair. "I'm not sure if I believe in a one true love, in the sense of everyone having a soulmate out there somewhere. That doesn't make me less passionate about you. Instead, it makes me feel even luckier to have found you. I just don't pin it all on destiny or fate. I don't believe some star fell from the sky or a baby angel shot us both with an arrow. I love you for who you are, because of who you are, not because of some fairy-tale spell. That's what I meant when I said that. There is no mystic force that compels me to love you, Sammy. I love you because of who you are—one hundred percent. Got it?"

"Yes, got it." I grimaced. "I'm so sorry. I know that trust shouldn't be an issue. You've never given me a reason to doubt you. I guess my mind just got a little out of control."

"If you'd just talked to me about it, we could have avoided all this." He rubbed his hand back through his hair. "I had no idea that you needed me to express my passionate side more often. I guess sometimes I fall back into friendship mode with you and I just expect that you know how much I love you."

"Maybe a shower will help me clear my head."

"You do that. I'll go get us some breakfast." He

started to turn away, then he paused. He pulled me close for a deep kiss. When he released me, I had to catch my breath. "I love you, Sammy."

"I love you too, Max."

The shower did help me sort out some feelings, but the tension was still there. I couldn't explain it. Even though Max had a perfectly rational explanation for everything, I was still on edge.

When he returned to the room with breakfast, we shared it along with strained conversation about our plans for when we'd be in Ireland.

"Do we need to talk more?" Max grabbed our suitcases.

"No, we're fine."

"Are you sure?" He met my eyes. "I don't care about the misunderstanding, I just want to know that you're telling me the truth."

"I'll be fine. It may take me a little time."

"Good. That's all I need to hear."

On our way out of the Inn, we were faced with yet another crowd of people.

"Come here." Max paused at the top of the steps and looked across the crowd at me.

"Max, we have to get to the airport or we're going to miss our flight."

"No. We can't go. Not yet."

"Why not?" I looked at him with exasperation. I wanted to get away from the initials, the crowds, and all memories of Valentine's Day.

"There's one more thing we need to do."

"Don't worry about it, Max. Things will be fresh in Ireland."

"No." He held my gaze. "We're not leaving London, we're not leaving these steps, until I know that you hear me."

"What do you want me to say, Max?"

"I don't want you to say anything. Just hold my hand." He held out his hand to me.

My heart lurched at the offer. With the tension that had built between us I wondered how he could want to hold my hand, but his soft smile indicated that he truly did.

I placed my hand in his palm. He gave it a light squeeze, then guided my hand over to the railing. He brushed my fingertips along the underside of the wood.

My heart beat faster at the sensation of freshly carved wood. "Max?"

CHAPTER 30

Max smiled and tilted his head toward the railing.

I glanced around to be sure that no one was looking. Then I ducked down and peeked underneath. Etched into the wood were our initials and the date of our first kiss.

I straightened up and looked into his eyes. "Max, you could have been arrested."

"So?" He drew me close to him. "I don't care about chains and bars, all I care about is you, Sammy. I need you to understand that. Maybe I'm not the most passionate man. I work with technology; I'd prefer not to analyze every painting I see. But you are my passion, Sammy. You've opened my heart and my mind in ways I never thought were possible."

"Max." I smiled at him.

"No, I mean it." He held my gaze and pressed my hand against his chest. "I need to know that you hear me, when I tell you this."

"I'm listening." I trailed my fingertips along his chest.

"Michelle was not my first kiss. She was not my first love. None of the women I dated were my first anything.

I didn't have my first kiss until the moment that I kissed you. You are the only woman I have ever, and will ever, love. I have shared my first everything with you. Have I kissed other women? Sure, but now that I've kissed you, I know what it's like to kiss the woman I love. The moment I found you—long before either of us ever knew what that meant—was the moment that I found the love of my life—the only one."

I leaned close to kiss him, but he pulled back and looked sternly into my eyes.

"Do you hear me?"

"Yes, I do." I gazed back into his eyes. "I hear everything. I love you too, Max."

"Good." He smiled and offered me a quick kiss. "Now every time someone wishes for good luck on this railing, they're going to get a little bit of ours too. Maybe our story isn't as dramatic, but it's just as passionate, Sammy. I would do whatever it took to get back to you and I will do whatever it takes to be with you. If for one second you doubt that, you need to tell me, because the thought of losing you…" He swallowed hard and shook his head. "I can't even think it, Sammy. Please promise me that you won't hide those feelings from me. Because all you have to do is tell me, and I'll spend the rest of my life proving my feelings for you."

"You don't have to prove it, Max." I sighed and wrapped my arms around him, relieved to be able to do so without the slightest qualm. "You don't have to prove anything to me. I trust you."

He kissed the top of my head and held me close. "Good. Because I need you to hear me right now." He pulled back and looked me straight in the eye.

"I do." I smiled into his shoulder.

"No, I mean really hear me. When I say run, we have to run."

"Huh?" I looked up in time to see one of the maids from the Inn as she pointed a police officer in our direction.

Quick fear rushed through me as I realized that she must have spotted Max when he'd carved our initials. My heart pounded. Was Max's romantic overture going to end in jail time?

"Run." He grabbed my hand and we ran down the steps of the Inn.

Luckily, we easily disappeared into the crowd of people who sought good luck from a railing. I laughed as we ran as hard and fast as we could. Maybe it was wrong for Max to carve our initials into the railing, but I knew why he did it, and it meant the world to me.

As long as we remained open with each other, and honest, we would never have to wish for good luck in our relationship. With Ireland waiting for us, our lives were magical, not just because of the travel and the chance to meet new people, but because of the passion that flowed between us, no matter the setting.

I hoped that I would leave a few things behind me in

London—my insecurity, some good luck for all the people that touched the railing, and a few new friends. I just hoped that I would be able to count Michelle among them, once I apologized for my dine and dash.

Maybe I was Max's first love, but she was his first best friend—and that was something I couldn't help but respect.

A NOTE FROM THE AUTHOR

Fictional character, Samantha Bradford and the Single Wide Female books are written for every woman out there who has struggled with their weight, self-esteem and any number of issues that we all face as we work to become the best versions of ourselves that we can be.

These books are meant to be light-hearted and fun, with the hope that they will also inspire you to make your own "bucket list" of sorts—and to REALLY live your life to the fullest, loving yourself completely as you do so.

Lillianna loves to hear from her readers and can be contacted via her website where you can also download a complimentary book.

LilliannaBlake.com

ALL TITLES BY LILLIANNA BLAKE

http://Amazon.com/author/lilliannablake
*Check the author page for current list of titles

Single Wide Female: The Bucket List
#1 Learn Pole Dancing
#2 Start a Blog
#3 Learn to Cook
#4 Create a Masterpiece
#5 Run a Marathon
#6 Go Skinny Dipping
#7 Start Online Dating
#8 Learn Yoga
#9 Be a Mentor
#10 Crash a Wedding
#11 Be a Movie Extra
#12 Join a Writing Group
#13 Enjoy a Spa Day
#14 Donate Blood
#15 Learn Poker
#16 Get a Tattoo
#17 Host a Dinner Party
#18 Publish a Book
#19 Walk Across Hot Coals
#20 Learn to Swim
#21 Learn to Meditate
#22 Quit My Job
#23 Learn to Salsa
#24 Fall in Love

Single Wide Female in Love

#1 The Date

#2 The Girlfriend

#3 The Fiancée

#4 The Wife

Single Wide Female Travels

#1 Sammy in France

#2 Sammy in Italy

#3 Sammy in Holland

#4 Sammy in England

Other Single Wide Female Titles

My Valentine's Day

St. Paddy's Day Disaster

A Bunny Tale

Sammy's Christmas List

Becoming Zara

*how the B.I.G. Girls Club came to be

B.I.G. Girls Club

The Rockstar's Girlfriend

The Former Model

Visit the author website at LilliannaBlake.com to get on the notification list for new releases and to receive a complimentary book to learn what inspired Sammy to begin her bucket list.